N
OF
THE
DEAD

# OTHER TITLES BY KEVIN WIGNALL

## Individual Works

*People Die*

*Among the Dead*

*Who is Conrad Hirst?*

*The Hunter's Prayer*

*Dark Flag*

*A Death in Sweden*

*The Traitor's Story*

*A Fragile Thing*

*To Die in Vienna*

*When We Were Lost*

## Short Stories

"The Window"

"Retrospective"

"A Death"

"Hal Checks Out"

# KEVIN WIGNALL

# THE NAMES OF THE DEAD

THOMAS & MERCER

Published by Thomas & Mercer, Seattle

www.apub.com

Amazon, the Amazon logo, and Thomas & Mercer are trademarks of Amazon.com, Inc., or its affiliates.

ISBN-13: 9781542000000
ISBN-10: 1542000009

Cover design: @blacksheep-uk.com

Printed in the United States of America

# THE
# NAMES
# OF
# THE
# DEAD

# One

Garrett and Norah hadn't arrived until just after midnight, exhausted by a day of travel delays, so the next morning they were eager to get out immediately after a late breakfast and see Granada. It was the second stop on their tour of Spain and Portugal, and this two-week vacation was their first overseas trip since spring break the previous year, so they were determined to soak up every minute of it.

The hotel was tucked away in the Albayzín, but a little distance from the busiest tourist streets. So as they climbed the stepped paths between white-walled houses, the morning stillness remained undisturbed by the few other visitors they encountered.

They had in mind to walk up to the Mirador de San Nicolás for the view over the Alhambra, but before they were even close they chanced upon a peaceful little square with a couple of cafés, a handful of people sitting at the tables of the one nearest them. It had the air about it of a refuge from the day ahead, from the heat that was already building in the pristine blue sky, from the hordes that would descend on the city over the next hour or so.

They didn't even need to discuss it. Norah looked at the café, glanced at Garrett, he nodded, and they took a table. There was an elderly English couple next to them, chatting quietly; a woman with a small boy sitting in comfortable silence; a young man with a bomb in the backpack that lay at his feet; a woman writing a postcard.

A waiter strolled out and they offered a "*Hola*," before lapsing back into English and ordering iced coffees.

Once he'd gone inside, Norah said, "This is so beautiful," her voice hushed to match the surroundings. The English couple had fallen into silence. Behind them, the little boy sucked at the straw in his drink and produced a slurping noise that made both him and his mother giggle.

A fair-haired family came into the square, a couple with a boy and girl of about nine or ten, and stopped in exactly the same place where the café had managed to snag Garrett and Norah. They seemed to be engaged in an inaudible discussion about whether or not to stay for a drink.

Garrett looked across at them but turned back to Norah when she said, "I could eat an olive right now. Is it too early for olives?"

He loved that she asked questions like that.

"Not unless they're in a martini."

She laughed, never dreaming those were the last words she would ever hear him say.

"Yeah, I think I'll have some olives."

Her words tumbled gently into the silence. The family continued its mute deliberation, the children patiently awaiting the decision. All was stillness around them, not even any noise from the café. Some olives. She would have some olives.

They had no real awareness of the explosion. A flash, almost lost against this overexposed morning. The instantly deafening bang. The pummeling of the air. The sense of everything hurtling in and flying away at the same time, of being crushed even as the world broke apart and scattered.

Garrett's physique, enhanced by two years of college football, didn't protect him, but it did protect Norah, shielding her from some of the blast. The old English lady survived for two days, the deliberating father for a week. The others were killed instantly, all hit with such flesh-rending force that it would be three days before the final death toll was firmly established.

Norah would lose her left leg just above the knee and suffer burns and other disfiguring injuries to her head, face, and right arm. For a week she would be kept in an induced coma, and it would be two more weeks before she was told that Garrett had died in the attack, though by that time she'd know it anyway.

And it would be two years before Norah O'Brien started to live some sort of life again, two years before she slowly began to accept her good fortune, that of the eight people in the café and the four standing nearby on that fine early-summer morning in Andalucía, she alone had survived.

# Two

"Do you ever think about the people you killed in southern Turkey?"

"Which people?"

"The people in the helicopter you shot down."

Most of the prisoners had group therapy. Wes was the only one whose first language was English so he got a one-on-one, as did some of the other non-French inmates.

The previous psychiatrist, Dr. Haddad, had retired just over a month ago. This was Wes's second session with the new one, Dr. Leclerc, who was young and slight and had a mane of glossy black hair—he was only a turtleneck sweater away from being the stereotypical French intellectual.

And now Leclerc was looking at him as if he thought Wes might be in denial about his reasons for being here. But at the risk of reinforcing that belief, Wes had to clarify one point.

"I didn't shoot it down. I mean, I killed them—I supplied the PKK with the weapon and the targeting information, and sure, I was there—but I didn't actually pull the trigger."

The clarification was received blankly.

"So how do you feel about that? Do you feel guilt, responsibility?"

"Responsible, yeah, sure; I targeted the wrong helicopter. Guilty? Not really, though I guess I wish it hadn't happened—I wouldn't be in here, my wife wouldn't have left me."

"You think your wife left you because of shooting down the helicopter? Or because you were sent to prison?"

"Does it matter?"

Wes smiled. It still amazed him that Rachel had been with him at all. They'd met at a security conference in Manama when he was twenty-eight and she was twenty-seven, and yes, he'd thought her beautiful, but more than that, he'd just enjoyed her company. They'd hit it off, but only as friends, and that's how it had stayed for the next five years—occasional chance meetings, the same buzz whenever he saw her, no inkling that she might be more than just a great person to hang out with.

Wes had run small offices in Ankara and Baghdad back then, with another one-man office down in Mardin in southeastern Turkey, run by Davey Franklin. But as ISIL had started to take up more of their time, Wes had made the decision to close Ankara and move to the Mardin office himself, along with a couple of the other guys.

He'd been sitting there at his desk one day, looking out at the view over the pale plains stretching hazily toward Syria, when Rachel had walked in, just like that. She'd been sent from the embassy in Baghdad to liaise with Wes's team.

*You're staying?*

*That's the plan*, she'd said. *If you have no objections.*

It seemed they'd both been pretty good at compartmentalizing, at treating what they had between them as purely platonic. Because the moment it had become viable they'd fallen for each other—and into bed—in a headlong rush. It had been pretty good for a while, too. For a while.

His smile fell away again.

"Why were you smiling?"

"I was smiling about something that's absolutely none of your business."

"Okay." It was obvious from his tone that Leclerc didn't think it was okay. "You're in prison and your wife left you. Are there any other reasons you regret what happened?"

"Of course. The wrong people died, but it's a volatile region—these things happen."

"You still maintain that the helicopter you shot down was not your intended target?" Leclerc looked down at his notes. "Two French aid workers from a charity which had directly accused the CIA of illegal acts in the region, plus two journalists and a UN observer who were investigating those very claims." He looked up again but Wes didn't respond. "Who was your intended target, if not them?"

"You know I can't answer that, Dr. Leclerc."

"Naturally." Leclerc glanced at his notes again but Wes suspected it was a feint. "So, if you targeted the wrong helicopter, was it in error or do you think you were manipulated . . . how you might say, set up? You know, you were a station chief—"

"I wasn't a station chief."

"But it's in the court record."

"No, it says I was running a team. It's not the same. I was never a chief of station. I wasn't even attached to a station."

"I understand, but my point remains. You were in an influential position, experienced in your field, not the kind of man to make mistakes. So again, if that helicopter really hadn't been your target, do you think you were set up?"

The smoke had still been rising from the wreckage, the PKK fighters still celebrating, when the call had come in to Wes from Harrod, telling him that there'd been some kind of mistake. Right in that moment he'd known in his gut it hadn't been a mistake at all, that he'd been fed the wrong intel intentionally, that someone had wanted him hung out to dry. At first he'd imagined the Turks being responsible, or even Grishko, his friend and GRU counterpart. It had been another few weeks before he'd worked out that he'd been set up by one of his own team.

"I don't know whether I was set up. It's clear you think so, though I can't imagine what that would have to do with this session."

"Really? In fact it's very interesting from a clinical point of view, that you express no feelings of resentment. And for what it's worth, yes, *if* the wrong helicopter was targeted, I think a setup is possible, given the nature of your work—"

"You don't know anything about my work."

Wes was aware of an edge of irritation in his own voice, and Leclerc smiled, apparently seeing it as some kind of breakthrough.

"What I do know is that you've been here for three years, and yet in that time your government has made not one attempt to have you transferred to an American prison, no government representative has ever contacted or visited you—nothing. And still you express no feelings of being abandoned or betrayed . . ."

Wes didn't respond, but Leclerc hadn't given up yet.

"It would be natural, no? To use the correct term, you *took one for the team*, and yet it seems your government has deserted you." Still getting no answer, he turned back to his notes for a few seconds, then looked up again. "This makes me concerned about how you'll cope in two years when you're released. Certainly, it doesn't seem you'll be welcomed with open arms."

Leclerc was onto something, but still seemed oblivious to what would most likely happen when Wes got out of here. The radio silence of the last three years had removed any doubt from Wes's mind. He was a liability now, and they would want rid of him. He was surprised they hadn't tried while he was in here, but he guessed it suited Sam Garvey better to wait until Wes was forgotten before killing him.

Yes, Sam Garvey had set him up, he was sure of that now. Wes's second-in-command, running the Baghdad office—supposedly his best friend too—but almost certainly rotten, removing anyone who became a risk or an obstacle. Wes had remained blind to it for so long, and yet from his current viewpoint, that blindness astonished him. Sam had set him up, and Sam would make sure he was a million miles away when someone else finally put a bullet in the back of Wes's head.

"You know, what concerns me, Dr. Leclerc, from a *clinical point of view*, is whether you're a prison psychiatrist at all, or if you've been sent in here by the DGSE to gather information on me and some of the other non-French prisoners."

"Not at all! I'm shocked you would say such a thing." Leclerc looked flustered rather than shocked. "I'm simply interested in exploring the absence of feelings I would expect to find in a case like yours, things like resentment or bitterness or—"

"I try to live in the moment, Dr. Leclerc. I'm in here for another two years—what good is resentment or bitterness to me? I did what I did, I am where I am. What other people have or haven't done is irrelevant. Dr. Haddad considered that a healthy mindset to have, under the circumstances."

"It can be. It can also be a sign of dissociation." Leclerc's doubts were evident, but then he sounded more positive. "But we've made good progress in this session. Perhaps next time we can explore the theme of denial."

"Denial?"

"Yes. When I inquired about the people you killed, your automatic response was to ask which people."

"Oh, that wasn't denial. I was just asking you to be more specific. I've killed plenty of people, and quite a few of them in southern Turkey."

"Then perhaps we need to talk about that."

"I don't think so. Don't confuse the difficult job I did with the man I am. I'm just a normal person."

"I'm not sure I believe that."

"Well, Dr. Leclerc, your beliefs are among the many things over which I currently have absolutely no control."

Wes stood, then picked up his book. He'd started taking along whichever book he was reading to his sessions with Dr. Haddad, and the old guy had ended up spending most of each session discussing literature or history rather than the state of Wes's psychological wellbeing. In their first session together, Leclerc hadn't even noticed the book Wes had with him, but this time he threw a curious glance at the cover.

"A history of the Qing Dynasty?"

"Yeah. I'm not sure why it interests me—maybe it's all the plotting and intrigue, betrayal, revenge. The Chinese knew a thing or two about exacting revenge."

Leclerc looked in danger of jumping out of his chair in excitement.

"I see, and does that appeal to your—"

"Relax, Dr. Leclerc, I'm messing with you. I'm not planning on revenge—I just like history."

Leclerc smiled humorlessly. And yet Wes was telling the truth. He'd always been good at compartmentalizing, and one thing he knew for sure was that, for the next two years, thoughts of revenge were utterly pointless.

# Three

They were painting in the garden, something they were managing more and more now that the weather was improving and summer was taking hold. As ever, for much of the time they worked without talking—they had enough daily opportunities for conversation that they never felt the need to fill the silences.

Wes looked across at Patrice's canvas on its easel, then back at the view in front of them. He liked the way Patrice always managed to capture the scene while simultaneously making his paintings richer, lusher than reality, as if a part of him were seeing a garden back home in the Congo rather than the French one in front of them. He noticed too, for the first time, that something else was always missing from the paintings.

"You never paint the fence."

Patrice looked at him, then looked forward, as if needing to be reminded that there *was* a fence.

"I like your paintings, Wes, but sometimes I think you paint *only* the fence."

"Because it's there, Patrice." This was no ordinary prison, designed as it was to house war criminals and other special cases, but it shared that one key characteristic of prisons everywhere. "The fence is everything."

"It's there. But it's not here—" Patrice tapped his head with a broad smile. "You see the fence, I see a Garden of Eden." Wes couldn't argue with that. They painted on for a minute or two, then Patrice added, "You know, Wes, we'll both be out of here in a couple of years, and I'll enjoy sitting in some nice place with you and some cold beers or even just coffee, somewhere even you won't see fences."

Wes imagined the two of them, living lives beyond this prison, meeting up occasionally to share those cold beers.

"I'd like that."

He meant it, too, though he doubted it would be that easy, and it was pretty much all his own fault. Grishko had told him a few times that he thought one of Wes's team was working with Omar Shadid, a Sunni strongman who specialized in trafficking drugs and weapons and people—people most of all. Wes had even begun to suspect it himself but he'd still never suspected Sam Garvey. As much as he'd liked Sam, he'd just never thought him that smart, and yet he'd outflanked Wes easily enough in the end. The lack of even a consular visit in the last three years confirmed something worse—that Sam had fooled everyone else, too.

In the light of that, meeting Patrice for drinks in two years was little more than a dream. And Leclerc really had no need to worry about how Wes might adapt to life outside. The radio silence said it all—Wes's time was already up.

"I had a session with Leclerc yesterday."

"And?"

"He seems more interested in getting information out of me than offering any kind of help."

"Yes!" Wes had apparently expressed something that had been niggling at Patrice. "In the group this morning, he asked me to talk about my crimes, again and again."

"What did you tell him?"

11

"I told him the Lord knows what I've done, and I reminded him that there will be rejoicing among the angels in heaven for this one sinner who repents."

Wes could imagine Leclerc's response to that.

"He asked me if I thought I'd been set up, betrayed by one of my own people."

Patrice said, "Did you tell him about the Garvey man?"

Wes smiled. Patrice pronounced "the Garvey man" as if he were a frightening character from a children's story, a far cry from the dull and dependable face Sam had actually presented to the world.

"I think Dr. Leclerc's a Freudian—I'm not sure how well he'd respond to me saying I believe the best man at my wedding set out to ruin my life."

"You chose your friend badly, that's all. But the CIA, they chose badly too, and they still think you are bad and he is good."

"I guess so."

Patrice looked deep in thought for a moment, his brush suspended in midair, before saying, "It's very wrong, that your government and your CIA treats you like this. You're an honorable man, Wes, and your people should treat you with honor. They should trust and respect you."

"I appreciate the sentiment, Patrice. Although, I *have* routinely discussed Agency operations with an African war criminal."

Patrice laughed. He laughed easily, with the air of a man who'd already been liberated. He turned back to his canvas then and added some extra strokes of vivid yellow to the shrubbery.

Satisfied, he said, "Look what the Lord has given us! Paradise." But when he turned to Wes, his face had grown contemplative. "You know Pavić died?"

"Who's Pavić?"

Patrice frowned. "You know him! The old man. The demon girl visits him."

12

Wes laughed now, knowing who he was talking about. He was a Croatian war criminal but Wes had only ever known him as "the General" because that was how the guards always addressed him. The girl was presumably General Pavić's daughter and Wes understood why Patrice thought of her as a demon, because she was painfully thin, with pale skin and unsettlingly dark eyes and white-blond hair.

"I didn't really know him."

"He was a good man."

Relatively speaking, thought Wes. Pavić, Patrice, and a few of the others, they were all good men in their own way, in each other's eyes at least, but they were all in here for doing horrific things—in the case of Pavić, that had included ethnic cleansing and the execution of prisoners, many of them civilians, many of them boys. Wes had done some pretty bad things too, but at least they'd been done for the right reasons, or what had seemed right at the time, anyway.

A door opened on the far side of the garden and Enzo, one of the guards, came out and started toward them, looking grim-faced. They both watched his approach, and then without being sure why, Wes started to clean his brush, sensing that his painting was over for the day.

Sure enough, as he got closer, Enzo looked at Wes and offered a sad regretful little smile.

"I'm sorry to disturb your painting, but, Wes, the Director needs to speak with you."

"Sure. He say what it's about?"

"No. I don't know."

He was lying, and Wes guessed that meant it was bad news from home that Enzo didn't want to break to him. Someone close had died, maybe one of his parents. Someone close. Someone close who, like his government, hadn't talked to him or contacted him in three years.

# Four

Enzo couldn't wait to make his escape once they reached Monsieur Dupont's modernist office with its wall of glass looking out over the neighboring forest. For his part, Dupont welcomed Wes like a priest greeting a parishioner in crisis.

"Wes, thank you for coming. Please, sit down. Can I get you a drink?"

"I'm good, thanks, Monsieur Dupont."

He remained standing, too, but as Dupont took his own place behind his sleek wooden desk he gestured again to the chair, an entreaty rather than a command, as if it mattered to him that Wes be seated for what he was about to say.

Wes sat and Dupont nodded sadly and said, "I have some terrible news. You heard about the terrorist attack in Spain yesterday."

Wes nodded through his confusion. He'd prepared himself for news from home, that one of his parents had died, or even one of his sisters, but the mention of Spain had thrown him off balance. Unless one of them had been on vacation . . .

"I saw it on the news, but what does it have to do with me?"

"It's best for me to tell you outright. Your wife—rather, your ex-wife—she was among the dead." Dupont looked down at a piece of paper in front of him. "Rachel. Rachel Richards. I imagine she changed her name again."

Rachel Richards. His ex-wife. Dead. These words made no sense; they seemed to refer to something unreal, something imagined or only vaguely remembered.

They'd married just nine months after she'd walked into his office in Mardin. Wes and Rachel had viewed it as whirlwind, others as hasty, and the low-key wedding had managed to alienate both families to some degree. They'd been married only a year before Wes's arrest. She'd initiated divorce proceedings immediately following his conviction and he hadn't contested it.

It was no time at all really, no lifelong romance, no world of common experience. They had liked each other for a long time, loved each other passionately for what now seemed a few sun-scorched weeks, and then it had ended. It already felt a lifetime ago, prison years being like dog years.

He had disciplined himself to put any love for her aside, to accept that he would never see her again, that she had stopped loving him. But he knew that he'd also carried something else within—a time capsule of other feelings and fanciful hopes, something that should have stayed buried for at least another two years.

The dislocation of having that time capsule cracked open now was too much. He no longer felt attached to his own body, as if his physical remains were dissolving into the plush chair. And he could hear Dupont's soothing voice, but as if through water, the words muffled and unformed.

And then, in a jarring moment of clarity, he heard Dupont say, "Wes? Are you sure you wouldn't like that drink?"

"She kept her name."

"What?"

"She didn't change it back, she never changed it in the first place."

Dupont nodded, but then stood and crossed the room with a look of concern, and Wes wondered how long the Director had

15

kept talking before Wes's response, how much of the crucial detail he'd missed. Was it even crucial? Rachel was dead—there was no more to it than that. He'd always thought he would die first.

Dupont placed a glass in front of him. Brandy. Dupont had one himself and drank most of it in one gulp as soon as he sat down. Wes leaned forward and picked up the glass, following suit. It burned his throat and made him feel instantly heady, the first alcohol he'd touched in three years.

"It's terrible, of course. She was on vacation. And the boy—"

"What boy?"

"I just told you. I thought you seemed confused—I should've waited." He looked angry with himself. "It's not just your wife, Wes. Your son is missing too. They can't say for certain yet, but naturally, they fear . . ."

Instantly, Wes was fully present again, his senses sharpened, his thoughts cutting through what he'd been told.

"How certain are they that it's Rachel?"

"Er, I . . ." Dupont moved the piece of paper on his desk as if that might help him. "I'm giving you only the information I was given by the US authorities. They're certain, I think. And your son . . ." He let the words fall away, apparently still nervous about how Wes was taking this piece of news, or fearful it wasn't sinking in at all.

"I don't have a son, Monsieur Dupont. Surely it's in my file. I don't have any children. Rachel and I, we were trying for a while, but . . . we didn't have a child."

"But . . ." Dupont looked down at the piece of paper again, then picked up the glass and drained the rest of his brandy. He pointed at the facts printed in front of him. "She was traveling with her son. They stayed in Madrid with a former colleague who works in the US embassy there, then they went off to tour southern Spain, your wife and your . . . It names you here as the father."

"No. She would have told me. If Rachel had a son, she must have met someone else after I came here. That's the only explanation." Wes felt stung by the prospect, and angry with himself for feeling stung—she'd desperately wanted a child and five years would have been too long, even if there had been any hope of them getting back together. Dupont nodded without any certainty, and Wes said, "How old was he?"

Dupont looked at the paper again, though Wes got the impression he knew the answer already.

"Two and a half years."

"Oh."

It was the worst answer when it should have been the best. They'd gone away for a week, once he'd known the arrest was coming—a week on the Turkish coast in which they'd been precipitously, impatiently happy. Could this child have been the result of that week, a child who was now dead, who he'd never known?

He reached forward and finished his brandy.

Dupont got up and fetched the bottle, pouring them each another hefty measure. Wes didn't know how he was meant to respond except with numbness. Even Rachel had come to feel unreal to him, so how was he meant to grieve for a child so intangible?

"He could be mine then. But he's dead."

"Missing."

"Unidentified isn't the same as missing, Monsieur Dupont. People don't go missing in suicide bombings."

Dupont appeared to acknowledge the point but looked preoccupied and sounded hesitant as he said, "I didn't hear this from the American authorities. I heard it from my brother-in-law who . . . well, who would know more than you or me. The scene is still very confusing—it's only twenty-four hours. At first they believed they had found the body of your son, near to your wife, but it wasn't him. And it seems so far that there are no more small children among the dead."

Wes felt a sickly nervous energy pulse through his body.

"So maybe he wasn't with her."

"I don't want to build your hope. It is, still, a very confusing picture. And it seems too unlikely—no?—that your wife would be on vacation with her son but not have him there with her when . . . Well, you understand."

He'd just found out Rachel was dead, that maybe he'd had a son, that maybe his son was also dead or, if not, missing in some mysterious way. So the simple answer was no, he didn't understand. He didn't want to hope, either.

Why had Rachel never told him? And why couldn't his own government do the bare minimum and send someone from the State Department to tell him face to face? Even without answers, those two questions seemed to sum up the totality of his abandonment.

When Wes said no more, Dupont shrugged and said, "Er, it may take a few days, a week, but there are plans to bring forward your release, on humanitarian grounds. Technically you're no longer next of kin, so officially you have no part to play in proceedings, but naturally—"

"No longer *her* next of kin. But if the boy's mine, I'd say I have a pretty good case for being *his*."

"Of course. I don't know the legal situation, but under law, the father must retain some rights."

"Do you have the name of the friend she was visiting in Madrid?"

Dupont shook his head regretfully. "You know how your government is. They keep such a tight lid on everything."

That was true enough, and a stark reminder of what an early release would really mean for Wes, that he would simply be bringing forward the day of his own reckoning. He'd long accepted that

Sam Garvey would try to kill him as soon as he got out, but it was unnerving to see that moment suddenly accelerating toward him.

It didn't help that the world had shifted beneath him. He'd always been relaxed about what might happen to him, and one of his few reasons for wanting to stay alive had been erased in the last few minutes. But it wasn't just about Rachel anymore, or even about Wes himself.

He could feel that sickly tingling still in his blood, of nervous anticipation and fear and emotions he couldn't even put a name to. There was a boy, dead or missing. Rachel's son, maybe his. There was a boy, and it was still too much of a revelation for Wes to understand exactly what that meant.

"What's his name?"

"Excuse me?"

"My son, what's my son's name?"

Dupont glanced at the paper again. "Ethan. Ethan Richards."

"That was her father's name."

And Wes stood, urgently, even though he had nowhere to go—as he'd said to Patrice, the fence was everything, and he felt that more than ever now.

"I need to find out, Monsieur Dupont. I need . . ."

"I understand. I'll do everything I can to get answers for you."

Wes nodded.

"Can I leave now?"

"Of course, Wes."

Dupont waved his hand toward the office door, and in his eyes was an acknowledgment that, in some way or another, Wes had already gone.

# Five

Wes went back to his own room first, his mind working through next moves, even as a stubborn background voice kept reminding him that there probably wouldn't *be* any next moves, that staying alive long enough to find the truth would be tough.

But that didn't mean he couldn't try. He'd had a shock, and this was the only way he knew how to deal with it, by turning it into a problem that needed to be solved. He had to stay alive and he had to find out where his son was. If he thought about it like that, it was no different to any field operation.

If he could get the name of the friend in Madrid, he could pay a visit and ask him or her. Except visiting an embassy official in Madrid wouldn't be easy either, and with a flash of resentment, he thought of this unknown friend of Rachel's, who knew more about his own son than he did. Rachel had been so desperate for a child, but Wes had wanted it too, and she'd known that.

He counted off three twenty-euro notes, then considered what might be the best approach and added another two. He went to Raphael's room and found him playing some crazy computer game.

Raphael paused it and only then looked to see who was standing in his doorway.

"Oh—hi, Wes." He was in his mid-twenties but looked about sixteen—his skin was so smooth that Wes wasn't convinced he even shaved yet, and in most prisons he would have had a hard time, but here everyone seemed to leave him alone, not least because he was the go-to person for fixing tech. "Problem?"

"Kind of. I wondered if you could get me a list of everyone who works at the American embassy in Madrid. I know that's a lot of people, but I need it."

Raphael became immediately animated, a response so deeply ingrained in his character that his eyes continued to dance even as he frowned and bit his lip.

"I don't know, man, I . . . You know, they're trying to extradite me already. If I got caught doing this, I mean . . ."

The kid was right. He was here for hacking into the websites of the CIA, FBI, NSA, and IRS, the latter being the one that had probably upset them most. Europe's human rights laws were protecting him for now, but if he did get extradited to the US he'd spend the rest of his life in the kind of prison that would show this one up for the summer camp it was.

Wes held out the money.

"So don't get caught." Raphael looked at the money in Wes's hand. "It's a hundred euros. I need this, Raphael, I wouldn't ask you otherwise."

"Okay. How soon do you need it?"

"They're letting me out early, maybe within a week, so I'd want it by then."

Raphael was calculating now, maybe seeing a way of doing this for Wes without worsening his own position.

"So, I think I can help. Before you leave, I'll give you a Gmail address and a password. I'll send the information to that address. But it's better . . . it's better for me if you don't access it until you leave."

Wes thought of asking him to search for the whereabouts of Sam Garvey, too, but he realized he'd be confusing two issues if

21

he did that. All he really had to do was stay out of Sam's way long enough to find out what had happened to his son.

*His son.* The strangeness of it kept washing over him in shallow waves.

Wes put the money down on the desk and shook Raphael's hand, then walked out into the garden where Patrice was just packing up. He stopped and looked as Wes approached.

"That explosion in Spain yesterday . . . My ex-wife was one of the people killed."

Patrice made a sign of the cross and said, "I'm sorry to hear it."

"Thanks. But there's an added complication."

"Then let's walk and talk."

Wes nodded and they left their easels behind, sauntering around the grounds as he recounted the conversation with Dupont. Despite the crimes Patrice had witnessed and perpetrated in his life, he seemed particularly disturbed by the possibility of Wes's son being missing, and angered on his behalf that he was only finding out about the boy now, when maybe it was already too late.

Finally he stopped walking and turned to look at Wes. "But your colleagues, if they did the things you said, and now you'll be released . . . will they try to kill you?"

"I think so. If I'm honest, it's probably what I'd do in the same situation."

"Are you concerned? You don't appear concerned."

"What's the point of being concerned? I either stay alive or I don't, I find him or I don't." He thought of Rachel—or rather, of the way she thought—and saw a more glaring truth. "Only trouble is, what good am I to Ethan anyway, if people are still trying to kill me? Probably no use at all."

They started walking again, the first few steps in silence, and then Patrice said, "I've never told you this story before, Wes, but perhaps I need to tell you now. When I was nine years old, I was

22

with my friend Emmanuel. We were playing at the river not far from our village. There was a waterfall. We weren't meant to play there—it was dangerous, with the waterfall and so many wild animals. Emmanuel thought he heard gunfire. I didn't hear it, but after a time he got so worried, we started toward home. That's when God's Own Army took us. We walked right into them."

"You never got back to the village?"

Wes was imagining their parents as dusk approached, starting to worry about the missing boys, but Patrice said, "No, but that was lucky for us, because God's Own Army had been there already and killed everyone. Our parents, our brothers and sisters, friends, all killed. *We* were the lucky ones. Because they decided we would make good recruits, and maybe they were right. A few days later, we came to another village. Two men they captured there, they made them kneel, then our captain gave me and Emmanuel each a gun— you know, like an assault rifle." He laughed, his voice booming. "It was *so* heavy. He told us to shoot the men, in the face. Emmanuel, he had to go first. But the man was crying, Emmanuel too, the captain was shouting, other men laughing, and at the last, Emmanuel, he couldn't do it. He lowered the gun as he fired." Patrice gave a Gallic shrug. "The bullet hit the man's stomach and he screamed and fell, and he died anyway, but a long death, and the captain, he hit Emmanuel so hard I thought he'd killed him too. So, when it was my turn, the man started to cry and plead with me, begging for his life, but I didn't listen and I didn't hesitate—I held up that gun, so heavy, and I shot him right in the face. Yes, I shot him in the face, and the captain, he patted me on the head and told me I was a good soldier and God would be proud. It made me want to try harder, and in the years after that, I killed and butchered and raped. Yes I did." He looked at Wes, gave another shrug, weaker this time in some way. "And five years later, I shot that captain in the face too, even as *he* pleaded and cried and begged for his life."

"Wow. That's something else, Patrice."

Wes had known a little of the crimes Patrice was in here for, but it was difficult to connect this story, with its intimations of what was to follow, with the man who'd become Wes's friend these last three years.

"What happened to Emmanuel?"

Patrice smiled, a little wistfully. "He didn't end up in prison."

Wes nodded, not sure he needed or wanted to hear the details.

"But this is why I told you this story. We were just boys, children. And that is why you must find your son. A child is an innocent thing, Wes, but soft like clay, and in the wrong hands . . . You have to find him, that is all. Because of what happened to me."

Wes knew it, too, and felt it at some primal level he'd never felt before. By the time he was released, maybe Ethan would have been found anyway and placed in safety—Rachel's father was dead and she'd had a fractious relationship with her mother, but she had a brother, Adam, with his own young family. And yet Wes knew that wouldn't be enough to satisfy him. Patrice was right: *Wes* needed to find him. He needed to stay alive, as tough as he knew that would be, and he needed to find his son.

"I'll do my best."

"I know you will, and if you allow it, may the Lord help and guide you."

Wes smiled. "Is he helping us here?"

"But of course! He helps us every day."

Wes nodded, accepting Patrice's remarkable faith, and wishing right now that he had some of it himself.

# Six

In the days that followed, Wes felt the presence of the fence more than ever. There was no more information, and the void filled with frustration and anger and self-recrimination.

In two more brief meetings with Dupont, the Director shared some of that frustration, explaining to Wes that each subsequent request for an update on the boy's whereabouts had been put into a holding pattern, which was where it had stayed. The news on the TV and internet was just as problematic, nothing more than a couple of reports claiming Ethan was now accounted for and hadn't been with his mother after all.

That apparent resolution had clearly been enough for the media, and the news cycle had moved on. Only a handful of conspiracy sites continued to run with the story, one saying he'd died in the explosion, another that he'd been kidnapped in the aftermath, all of them suggesting the truth had been hushed up for various implausible reasons.

In the end, Wes stopped looking at the news sites altogether, and spent more time on his bed, staring up at the ceiling, turning over in his mind the things he needed to do, the obstacles that might be put in his way, turning over the events that had put him here. Now that he was close to getting out he started to feel the stirrings of resentment, which might have made Dr. Leclerc happy but only made Wes uneasy—this was no time to be thinking about himself.

A week after hearing the news he was lying on his bed when someone knocked on the open door. He looked up and saw Fabien, a young guard who always had the air about him of being stoned.

Languidly, Fabien said, "Hey. You have a visitor. So . . . you need to come?"

Wes jumped up. "Okay, let's go."

He guessed it would be someone from the embassy, come to talk him through his release and what would happen, maybe even update him on his son. A part of him even hoped it might be the kind of visitor he'd been waiting for these last three years—someone who'd apologize for his treatment, welcome him back into the fold, offer assistance.

Fabien led him to a part of the prison Wes didn't know, and as he opened a door onto a long quiet corridor, he said, "This is the visitor suite, for private visits—you know, like with your lawyer, or . . ."

He paused, looking for the end of his own sentence, and Wes said, "I've never been here before."

Fabien smiled goofily as if Wes had cracked a joke. "You never had a visitor before." He walked him to a door halfway along the corridor and pointed to it. "In there. I'll be out here."

Wes nodded and pushed open the door. Maybe the room was on the same side of the prison as the Director's office because the windows looked out onto what appeared to be the same stretch of forest. There were a few low chairs, and a coffee table with a box of Kleenex on it.

The suited man who'd come to see him was looking out of the window, but he turned now and Wes took a moment to place him, then another to overcome his immediate and visible disappointment. They'd only met once before, so the confusion was understandable, and the disappointment maybe even more so, because this clearly wasn't a welcome back into his previous life.

"Hey, Wes."

"Adam."

Rachel had worked at keeping fit and had been curvy in a healthy way. Her brother had about forty pounds in all the wrong places, thinning hair, a sheen of sweat on his brow. He was two years younger than Rachel and looked ten years older, or had done until a week ago, when age had stopped meaning anything at all.

They shook hands and Wes said, "I'm sorry for your loss."

Adam nodded his acceptance, clearly feeling no need to recip- rocate the sentiment, then gestured to the chairs as if this were his office and Wes his guest.

Once they were sitting, Adam said, "I had to come over to Europe to . . . well, to arrange things. I thought it was the least I could do while I was here to come and pay my respects, even though you weren't together anymore."

"I appreciate that."

Adam appeared not to hear him. "I thought I might have to identify the body, but apparently they had to use her dental records. She was caught pretty bad." He choked on the final word and sat for a moment, his jaw clenched. "Anyway, the State Department's been really helpful, the Agency too, considering she didn't work for them anymore."

"What do you mean, she didn't work for them anymore?"

Adam looked at him, lost, his face glistening, and Wes couldn't tell if it was just sweat or if he'd shed a few tears.

"I only found out myself two days ago. She went part-time when she had the baby, but she quit completely six months ago."

"So you haven't been in touch with her?" Adam looked embar- rassed, or hurt. "You knew she had a baby?"

"Yeah. It was difficult, you know. She was so close to Dad, so after he died, then the whole business of . . . well, of marrying you, and living in the Middle East and all."

Wes smiled, because he and Rachel had laughed about it, how their respective families had frowned upon the match despite knowing very little about it, maybe even *because* they'd known so little—neither had been able to tell their relatives what their new partner really did for a living.

But right now, Wes didn't care about the internal tensions of the Richards family.

"Where's the boy, Adam?"

Adam shook his head, the grief washed with confusion now. "We don't know. No one knows. She was visiting someone in Madrid, I don't know who, some former colleague. Ethan was with her. When she left, Ethan was with her. But somewhere between there and Granada, he disappeared. Why would she do that? She didn't know she was gonna die. She was on vacation. The State Department thinks she left him with friends, but we don't know who or where."

"If she left him with friends, why haven't they come forward?"

"We don't know that either. The State Department's assured us they're doing everything they can, and they're managing to keep a lid on it, but . . . it's a desperate situation, just . . ." He shook his head by way of ending the sentence.

"Is he mine?"

"Of course. I mean, I'm pretty sure. I haven't seen Rachel since he was born. Only spoke to her a few times. You know we . . ." He looked in danger of breaking down, but managed to regroup and looked up again. "They told me you're listed on the birth certificate."

"She would have needed my approval for that. For a passport, too." But even as he spoke, and as Adam looked lost in response,

Wes knew that Rachel would have known ways around those rules. The only thing he still didn't know was why. "You have any pictures?"

"Yes." Adam reached into his jacket but stopped short. "Not on my phone. I have two on my computer at home. She sent one when he was born, another on his first birthday. I could email them to you."

"Does he look like me?"

"Mom thought so, from the pictures anyway. She said he looked just like you." Implicit in Adam's tone was the suggestion that Rachel's mother hadn't considered that a good thing. "I couldn't tell who he looked like. But he was a cute kid."

Wes fought an urge to correct Adam for using the past tense, and said simply, "Well, I appreciate you coming."

"Like I said, I felt I owed you that much. Um . . . the funeral service, it'll be next week. I know the warden said you might be out—"

"No, I won't be there. It wouldn't be right even if I could." Wes stood up and Adam took that as his cue to do the same. "Whatever happens . . . Well, nothing, I guess. But thanks for coming, Adam."

Adam nodded and they shook hands and he left. Wes turned and looked out over the forest. Now that he considered it properly, he was certain Dupont's office was above this one—the same view, but a floor higher. The realization felt like a small mystery solved, which seemed important in some way, maybe only because nothing else was any clearer.

But Ethan was alive—that was the key thing, above Wes's own fate, even above his hopes of finding him. Their son was alive, so that would have to be Wes's starting point.

# Seven

In the end it was another full week before Wes's early release came through. He assumed he'd missed Rachel's funeral in that time. He didn't miss any more news about their son, because there wasn't any. As far as the wider world was concerned, Ethan Richards was no longer news. It was as if he'd ceased to exist. And given that Wes had received no more visitors, he became more convinced than ever that the same fate was planned for him.

Patrice came to see him in his room just before Wes left. He stood, filling the doorway, and looked down at the packed bag with a satisfied smile, maybe picturing those future meetings over drinks that he imagined in the outside world.

"What will you do?"

"If I stay alive long enough?" Patrice shook his head, dismissing the question, and Wes continued. "I'll look at Raphael's list, then I guess I'll head to Madrid. I don't know much, but I know Ethan didn't die in that attack, so he has to be somewhere, right? I mean, someone must know."

He wondered if Adam had heard any more, but Adam hadn't been in touch since his visit, not even to send the pictures he'd promised. Wes doubted he'd hear from him again, and as frustrated as he was that he still didn't know what his own son looked like, he didn't much want to be part of Rachel's family anyway.

"You'll find him."

"I'll try."

Patrice stepped into the room and held out an envelope. Wes took it and looked at the address on the front.

"I have friends in Lisbon. If you need anything—weapons, money, anything at all—go to this address and ask for this man. The letter inside is from me to him. He'll help."

"I appreciate it."

He slipped the letter into the side pouch of his bag.

"There's something else. I know you're not a religious man, but I want you to take this." Patrice often had a bible in his hand as he walked around the prison, and so Wes only noticed now that the leather-bound volume in Patrice's hands wasn't the book he normally carried. "When I was sent to the prison at home, then Paris, then The Hague, always I carried this to defend myself, in the body and in the soul, but I never needed it. Now it's more use to you, I think."

"Okay."

"It doesn't matter that you don't believe. There's still so much for you to find inside." He pointed to the two yellow ribbon bookmarks that were attached to the spine and which nestled among the pages. "Here is your guide. And here is your sword of truth. Be sure to look at both before you leave this prison, and God will help you find a way, Wes."

This was no time for a theological debate, and he was touched that his friend had so much belief on his behalf. He took the book and shook Patrice's hand.

"I don't care what the world says: you're a good man, Patrice. If I do live, we'll have that drink one day."

"We will, I have faith."

Enzo appeared in the doorway behind them, and said, "Wes, your car is on its way, so we have to go now."

He nodded, said goodbye to Patrice, and then found himself for the last time in Dupont's office. Dupont wasn't there, so Wes sat and looked at the bible Patrice had given him.

He pulled at the first yellow bookmark, which opened onto a page near the back of the book, the New Testament. It was the parable of the lost sheep, the symbolism a little heavy for Wes's tastes, but then he noticed that Patrice had used a pencil to mark out a line of text lower down the page—*I say unto you, there is joy in the presence of the angels of God over one sinner that repenteth.*

He didn't think the underlining was for his benefit. It was more or less the same sentiment Patrice had expressed to Leclerc. Flicking through the pages, he noticed other favorite passages underlined here and there, and smiled at the thought of his friend taking comfort from these ancient words.

Wes pulled the second bookmark then, but it opened onto the blank pages inside the back cover. There was nothing to see there. And yet Patrice had clearly pointed to both of them—*this is your guide, this is your sword of truth.*

Then he noticed that this bookmark wasn't attached to the binding but to something hidden inside the spine of the book. He tugged at it, and it came away from the bible, pulling a piece of metal with it. It was a T-bar across the top where the yellow bookmark was tied off, with the vertical forming a single spike the full length of the spine.

Wes smiled as he slipped it back carefully into its hiding place. *That* was his sword of truth. Patrice had carried his armed bible through several prisons, always ready to pull that blade, and yet he'd never been required to use it. Wes's moment would undoubtedly come, sooner rather than later, and knowing the nature of the threat he'd face, he'd have preferred a gun, but he was still grateful to have any weapon at all.

He heard the sound of approaching voices; or rather, one voice—Dupont's. Wes stood as the Director came into the room with another suited man behind him. He was around thirty, maybe, short dark hair, a pallid face that made him look like a sickly child.

"Wes, this is Mr. Pine from the US embassy in Paris."

"Zach Pine," he said, holding out his hand with a geniality that didn't extend to his eyes. It was a show, for Dupont's sake, and Wes could see exactly what Zach Pine thought of him.

He looked familiar—that pale and spectral face had somehow lodged in Wes's mind—but Wes didn't know him and had definitely never worked with him. What Wes did know, what he could feel in his gut, was that Zach Pine had been sent here to kill him.

And it was true that he'd known or suspected for three years that this would happen, but the betrayal stung all the more in this moment of confirmation. After all that he'd given, and all that he'd lost, still they wanted to take what little he had left.

# Eight

Dupont dealt with a couple of formalities, then shook Wes's hand. A guard came in to escort them out, but before they left, Pine reached into his inside pocket and pulled out a small bundle, holding it out for Wes to take.

"Nearly forgot. This is your passport, bank and credit cards— we've set everything up so that you can get back to normal as soon as possible."

Wes looked at the packet, and took it even though he knew what was going on here. They'd kill him before he got anywhere he might use those cards, but someone would use them in the coming weeks before destroying them, creating the impression that Wes had simply gone off the grid.

"Thanks, Zach. Good to know I haven't been abandoned."

"That's not how we work. You know that."

Dupont was looking on, mesmerized, but when he caught Wes's eye he said, "Bye, Wes. I hope not to see you again." The joke was well worn but he laughed as though he'd only just thought of it.

Wes shook his hand again, conscious it might be the last friendly interaction he experienced, and then he and Pine followed the guard out of the office.

As they walked, Wes said, "What happened to my son?" Pine looked at him, uncomprehending. "The terrorist attack in Granada? My ex-wife was killed. My son . . ."

"Oh, sorry, of course. I get you. I'm not really in the loop on that, but I'm sure someone else will give you more information later. The last I heard, they think he's with friends."

"But they don't know for sure?"

Pine shrugged, reinforcing his claim that he was out of the loop on this subject. The more Wes looked at him, the more familiar he seemed.

"You used to work with Peterson, didn't you, Zach?"

"I've worked with a lot of different people." The charm was fading now as they got closer to the external doors.

"You never worked with me. Until now."

Pine looked at the guard walking along the corridor in front of them and lowered his voice as he said, "We're just transport. We're taking you to a rendezvous point to meet George Frater. He'll take you back to Paris."

George Frater had been Associate Deputy Director at Langley, and Wes's direct superior.

"Why didn't he come and meet me himself?"

"I would've thought that was obvious. This whole case has been radioactive." Pine turned briefly and tried a sympathetic smile, not quite pulling it off. "We didn't abandon you, but we had to make it look that way."

"I know."

What Pine couldn't know was that George Frater had been one of the very few people from the outside world to contact Wes during his time in prison. Six months into his stay, Wes had received a handwritten note from George, sent via Director Dupont, in which he'd apologized and told Wes about his early (and most likely forced) retirement. So it was extremely doubtful that George Frater was sitting twiddling his thumbs anywhere nearby.

There was a black car waiting outside for them. Wes could see a driver, but as the trunk popped open, another guy climbed out of the passenger side and opened the rear door.

Pine took Wes's bag from him, and as he put it in the trunk he said to the waiting man, "Pat him down."

Wes looked at him. "Seriously?"

"Protocol. You know, in case you went nuts while you were in there." He tried what Wes assumed was meant to be a charming smile, but then turned back to the other guy. "Pat him down, Skip."

Wes wasn't sure if Skip was the guy's name or a familiar term that Pine used for everyone, like "pal" or "buddy." Skip was sandy-haired and thick-necked and a good three inches taller than Wes. He also avoided looking him in the eye as Wes held his arms out.

Once he was done he took the bible from Wes's outstretched hand and flicked through the pages. And as he handed it back he finally looked at him and gave a curt but respectful nod toward the book. A believer, thought Wes, and he wondered how Skip would justify to himself what they were planning to do.

Pine got in behind the driver, Wes behind Skip, and they set off along the quiet road through the forest that bordered the prison on two sides. When he'd been brought here three years earlier, the guard had told him it was the northern edge of a large national park, as if he'd be spending his weekends hiking the forest paths.

Wes couldn't tell what the driver was carrying. Skip was right-handed and wearing a shoulder rig. Pine was right-handed too, but wearing his gun at the waist at three o'clock—not the best choice for easy access sitting in the back of a car. None of them seemed inclined to speak.

After a minute or two, Wes said, "Where's the meet?"

"Not far."

"I'm surprised Sam Garvey didn't come to meet me."

"I don't know anyone by that name." Wes noticed the driver glance at him in the rearview before quickly looking away again, the tiniest tell that seemed to inadvertently acknowledge Pine's lie. All three of them were nervous—Wes sensed that now.

"Sam was my second-in-command. But I guess George didn't want him here."

"I guess not."

They'd probably only driven a mile or so when the driver slowed and turned right onto a track that headed deeper into the forest. Wes noticed some subtle movement in Skip's broad shoulders, then heard the faint but unmistakable sound of metal on metal as he attached a silencer to his gun. Wes had to wonder how necessary that was out here, but he didn't have time to ponder.

The track had become rough in places, bumping them about, but the driver was still doing a decent speed, as if he, too, was eager to get on and get this done. Wes used the rocking motion to mask his own movement as he tugged on the bookmark and eased the T-bar free of the bible's spine.

He wrapped his fingers around the T-bar either side of the stiletto blade, readied himself, then used his other hand to release his seatbelt. An alarm sounded on the dash, alerting the driver to the unfastened seatbelt, but Wes was already moving, swift, determined, striking before anyone had registered the alarm or who'd caused it.

Wes threw a hard swiping punch into Pine's throat with the side of his left hand, and simultaneously rammed the knife into the side of Skip's neck, jabbing it down violently, three or four times in quick succession. Skip screamed, the driver shouted something, panicked. A punch smashed into the side of Wes's head and as he turned he could see Pine was dazed but still fighting, reaching

37

for his badly placed firearm—a second punch would have been smarter.

Wes let go of the blade, leaving it deep, and latched on to Pine's gun as he pulled it clear of its holster. Pine still had his seatbelt on, so Wes lunged, head-butting him, pushing the gun aside and wedging Pine's finger against the trigger. Three deafening shots tore into the back of the driver's seat.

The car immediately accelerated and Wes could feel and vaguely see that they'd veered off the track, but there was hardly time to brace himself before the collision. He was hurled into the back of the passenger seat, airbags exploded, glass shattered, an oddly musical sound in the midst of all that noise.

Pine was restrained by his seatbelt, protected from the jolting shock of the impact, but Wes's grip had been the more determined, and he was the one now holding Pine's gun. Pine started to say something, but Wes shot him in the chest and threw a quick glance over his shoulder to make sure the others were dead, before turning back to see Pine shutting down, his eyes locked in some final confusion.

Wes looked down at his own right hand, cut and bleeding from gripping the blade. He turned gingerly in the confined space of the seat and pulled the knife from Skip's neck, the exit finding a gristly resistance he hadn't noticed as he'd stabbed it in.

He wiped the blade clean on Pine's jacket, then found the bible where it had fallen into the well between the seats and carefully slipped the blade back into its hiding place inside the spine. And in that moment his heart was more full of gratitude for Patrice than it had ever been for anyone.

# Nine

It wasn't until he got out of the car that he realized what a bad state he was in—his chest and shoulders felt crushed, his arms and legs ached, the cuts on his hand burned. Looking at the car, though, he felt like he'd gotten off pretty lightly: it was a crumpled mess of metal and airbags, suggesting the impact speed had been higher than Wes had realized.

He set to work, fighting past the airbags to get to the bodies. The driver had been unarmed, but Wes found a clean handkerchief in his inside pocket, so he wiped the blood from his hand as best he could, then tied the handkerchief around it. He took their phones and IDs, retrieved the two guns and two spare magazines.

The trunk had popped on its own, his bag the only thing in there. He opened it and put the guns and magazines in. He was about to put the phones in, too, but he wasn't sure what use that would be, other than providing them with a way of tracing his movements. He tossed the phones and the IDs, and set off back along the track, his bag in one hand, the bible in the other.

Within a few steps he was already in trouble. He'd twisted his ankle in the crash, probably as he'd been thrown into the back of the passenger seat. He didn't think he'd broken it, but it hurt to put weight on it. He swapped the bag and the bible over to lessen the weight on the side of the bad ankle, but the straps made the cut hand scream in pain.

He wouldn't be able to walk far, he knew that much, and he didn't know how long it would be before someone called to check in with Pine. They'd planned to kill him somewhere within this forest, which meant Pine's superior, whether Sam Garvey or someone else, would be expecting confirmation any time now. How long before they guessed something was wrong? How long before they sent backup?

Wes stopped walking. Listened. A bird made a strange menacing call from somewhere deep beyond the crash site behind him, but Wes could hear something else, too—a car, out on the road. It couldn't be backup, not this soon, which meant it had to be a civilian, a passerby, and he didn't know how long it would be before another came by on such a remote road.

He picked up his pace, into a hobbled limping run, his breath catching inside his bruised chest, darts of pain coming alternately from his ankle and his hand. Each step made him want to stop, to collapse and curl up by the side of the track, but he kept running. He ran because he knew that remaining alive could most likely depend on whether he got to the road in time.

He kept running even as he staggered from the track onto the smoother road surface, and felt a surge of relief as he turned and saw the vehicle still approaching. He dropped the bag to the ground, flexing the hand inside his makeshift bandage, relishing the pain of it in some way.

The car was close enough now for him to see that it was a dark blue Mercedes G-Class, the kind that looked like a utilitarian off-roader but came with a six-figure price tag. Wes had seen plenty of them in the past, usually driven by the wives or girlfriends of gangsters and soccer players.

He could see that the driver was alone, a woman, fair-haired. But then the car stopped, fifty yards short of where he was standing. Wes waved with the hand that held the bible, then bent down and picked up his bag before setting off toward her.

He waved again, fearing she might reverse and drive away. But, instead, the door opened and she got out. Wes recognized her instantly: Pavić's daughter, the one Patrice had called the demon girl.

And, once again, Wes could see Patrice's reason for thinking of her in that way. She was wearing a skinny white long-sleeved top and skinny black jeans—"skinny" being the operative word because she was incredibly thin. But it was the almost-total absence of color in her face and hair that made her look so otherworldly. Her eyes were dark, but that looked even stranger set within those alabaster features, tipping her androgynous looks into something almost alien. He guessed she was about thirty, and that Pavić had been well into middle age when she was born.

"Hi! Hello, can you help? I've been in an accident."

Even as he said it, he knew it was the kind of thing he'd have warned a daughter about—strange men on desolate roads claiming to have been in an accident.

She was standing behind the open door, as if using it for protection, and he could see now that she looked afraid, so afraid that he couldn't understand why she hadn't just driven around him, why she didn't get back in now and drive off.

He waved again, the bible feeling heavy suddenly, his energy falling away. "Hello. You speak English? I just need a ride, into Bordeaux, or any place nearby." She shook her head and backed away a couple of paces. "I won't hurt you. I don't mean any harm. I just need a ride."

She was taking another step backward now for every hobbled step he took toward her.

She called out, "Take it. I've left the key in there."

"*What?* No, I'm not stealing your car! I need a ride, that's all. I couldn't drive it if I wanted to—I've hurt my ankle, cut my hand. I was in an accident, back there in the forest." She stopped moving, but maybe only because he'd reached the SUV and stopped moving himself. "I've seen you in the prison. You're General Pavić's daughter." She remained silent, her chalk features impossible to read. "I'm sorry for your loss."

She stared back, glanced at the trees, back to him, and he thought he detected suspicion in her voice when she said, "You were in a taxi?"

"No." He didn't know why, except perhaps that he knew her father had been a soldier serving time as a war criminal, but he decided to gamble on the truth. "The three men who collected me from the prison, they tried to kill me, so I killed them. The car ran into a tree." There was no response, the same blank stare. "I had to kill them. They would've killed me otherwise."

"Are you a soldier?"

"Kind of."

At first he thought she might not respond again, but then she started talking and looked in danger of not stopping. "Sometimes soldiers have to kill other soldiers. It's sad but it must be. And they get hurt. I have a first-aid kit in the car. But you can't put your bag in the trunk space; it's too full already. It can only go in the back seat."

"Thank you." He didn't know what else to say, and feared he might easily say the wrong thing if he did add anything.

She appeared to weigh up his thanks, then started walking toward the back of the SUV, veering slightly to maintain some small distance between herself and Wes, as if he were a chained dog that couldn't be trusted.

Wes opened the rear passenger door before she could change her mind, and dropped his bag and the bible onto the seat. He moved around to the back then, where she'd opened the tailgate, and he saw what she meant, because the trunk space was full, a couple of large suitcases, various bags and boxes—he guessed she'd been more or less living near the prison and now that her father was dead, she had no reason to remain.

She stepped back toward the edge of the road, so he smiled and said again, "Thank you." He held out his bandaged hand. "I'm Wes."

She stared down at it, and as his own eyes followed her gaze he could see the white handkerchief was already soaked through with blood, but it wasn't horror at the wound that apparently disturbed her.

When she looked up again, she said, "I don't like to touch people."

"Okay. That's okay. So . . ." He lowered his hand, but then lifted it in a wave. "I'm Wes. Hello."

She looked shyly amused by that and said, "Hello."

"What's your name?"

"Mia Pavić. I'm getting the first-aid kit now. Your hand is hurt."

"Yeah, thanks."

He took a step back, giving her enough space that she wouldn't feel threatened. She started moving things about, lifting one bag out and placing it on the road, throwing cautious glances in his direction as if she feared he might still try something.

She picked up a box and looked ready to place it on the ground too, but hesitated and then held it out to Wes.

"Hold this, please." He took it from her, being careful to avoid making contact. "It's my father."

He wasn't sure how to respond to that one, but he didn't need to. She went back to rummaging in the back of the SUV as he stood there holding the cremated remains of General Pavić. A moment later she held out the first-aid kit and they swapped the two boxes.

She closed the tailgate again and they got into the car.

Wes opened the first-aid box on his lap as he said, "I really appreciate this."

"It's important to wear a seatbelt." He looked at her, trying to read her expression, her tone, trying to work out what it was that was a little off—she was like a highly advanced android that was still one percent short of being convincing. "We might be in an accident."

"Of course."

He put the belt on, even though, ironically, he alone hadn't been wearing a seatbelt in the accident that had just happened. But then, it hadn't been the impact with the tree that had killed the other three.

She drove on as he cleaned his hand again and bandaged it properly, wincing all the time with the shallow stinging of the cuts.

He'd almost finished when Mia said, "You want to go to Bordeaux."

"That's right. I should be able to get a train there, head south."

"You're the black man's friend."

The change of subject threw him momentarily, but then he said, "I am. His name's Patrice."

"I don't like black people."

"Wow. *Okay.*"

He could see that she was frowning, and then she hit the brakes, so abruptly that the first-aid kit nearly flew off his lap and the seat-belt dug across his chest, a crushing reminder of how bruised he was from the crash.

He feared she was about to tell him to get out of the car, but once they were stationary, she looked across at him.

"I used the wrong word. I haven't been speaking English much lately. I meant, I don't *know* black people."

"Oh. Good. That's easier to fix."

"It's important to be accurate."

"Sure, particularly around subjects like that." Wes was struggling to keep up. She was clearly on some kind of spectrum, but he wasn't sure which one or if he was fully equipped for dealing with it. He looked around. "Can we . . . drive on now?"

"Yes." It still seemed to take her a moment to register that he meant right now, but once they were moving again, she said, "You want to go to the railway station."

"That's right."

"Will you be late for your train, because of the accident and killing the three men?"

He smiled to himself, at the way she mentioned the killing of people almost in passing, the kind of everyday incident that might result in anyone missing a train.

"I don't have a ticket for a particular train. I'll see about that when I get there."

"That's good. It means we can't be late."

She fell into silence and he followed suit, staring out at the forested northern edge of the national park that had been his home for the last three years, and the home of Mia's father, too. Patrice would have seen a paradise here, where there was none.

He noticed she drove with a relaxed confidence, and that was how it was all the way into Bordeaux, suggesting maybe she'd been staying there during her father's imprisonment and that this journey was a familiar one to her.

As they approached the main concourse at Saint-Jean, she seemed unsure of herself for the first time, but Wes pointed and said, "Pull into that side street over there." She turned into the narrow street, driving halfway along it before finding a space to park.

"Okay, well, thanks again, Mia. I really don't know what I'd have done if you hadn't shown up when you did."

"Which train will you take?"

"I don't know yet, I'm . . . I'm headed to Madrid."

She looked delighted by his answer. "Oh! Spain is very beautiful at this time of year. I went there two times, but never to Madrid. It's a nice city, I think."

"I'm sure it is. I'm not going on vacation or anything, but . . ."

He wasn't sure how to end the conversation, but then, as if she'd hit on something obvious, she said, "*I* could drive you."

He laughed, then immediately regretted it because she'd been serious and looked confused by his response.

"To Madrid? Mia, I can't let you do that. I just met you, for one thing, and it's got to be five hundred miles."

"It's more than that to Croatia."

"That's where you're headed?" She nodded. "But then, Madrid's in the wrong direction."

"I have . . ." She ground to a halt and looked despondent, and he didn't want to hear what words he guessed had dried in her throat—probably that she had no one waiting for her, that in some way Wes might be as much of a lifeline to her as she had been briefly to him. He felt for her, but it was a complication he could do without. "I could drive you. People tried to kill you, but if I drive you, no one will know where you are. That would be good, I think."

She had a point, but not enough of one.

"Okay." She smiled, but it faltered as he said, "I have to go into the station anyway. I need to take as much money as I can out of an ATM—if they trace it, they might think I took the train. But I'll be back."

His explanation was superficially logical enough, and that seemed to satisfy her.

"I'll wait."

46

"Yeah, sure." He got out, then opened the back door and pulled his bag out. "I'm taking this so I don't look suspicious. They might spot me on CCTV."

She nodded, once again accepting his logic without any apparent suspicion that he might be lying. He thought about saying something else, but instead he closed the door and made his way to the station.

And it was only as he started walking that he realized he'd left his bible on the back seat. He felt bad about that, a sense that he owed it to Patrice to read a little of it, even as he hoped he wouldn't need to use it again as a weapon.

He had guns now, but even that thought jarred and unsettled him, reminding him of the real dilemma he faced. He had to find Ethan, but at the same time he had to stay ahead of Sam and somehow go above Sam to whoever it was at Langley who could remove the target from Wes's back. In the face of that challenge, killing three CIA officers in a French forest probably hadn't been the best start.

# Ten

He found an ATM and took as much money out on the cards as the machine would allow. He looked up at the boards then, spotting a train to Hendaye on the border. That would be the easiest thing, but he had to think about the way his countrymen and former colleagues would anticipate his every move.

He'd just killed the three men they'd sent to kill him, so they knew he'd go on the run, they knew he'd take all the cash he could and then ditch the cards. Maybe they'd expect him to show up in Switzerland at some point, though he didn't think anyone knew exactly where he kept his account. Maybe they'd expect him to head to Paris, a big enough city to disappear in, and with plenty of transport links to leave by when the time came.

But they also knew what he'd learned in the last two weeks, so above all they would expect him to go to Spain, and that was tough, because it was what he had to do. And he feared his senses would have been dulled by the last three years, that they might predict his next moves better than he could himself.

There were a few trains showing up on the boards for Paris, plus the one for Hendaye and a few others for cities from which he could make for Barcelona and head south that way. He'd never been on the run before, but he'd been party to a pursuit often enough and he knew the array of journeys in front of him would be all too easy to read.

The only option that would buy him the vital time he needed was the one he'd instinctively ruled out. They'd be expecting him to turn up in Madrid, so he wouldn't be surprising anyone by going there. But he could at least add uncertainty to the details by keeping them guessing about the means and timing of his arrival.

He made his way to a ticket booth and bought a ticket to Narbonne, once again using the credit card Pine had given him. Then he went to another booth and used cash to buy a ticket for the TGV to Paris in just over an hour. It probably wouldn't fool them for long, but it would make their job more complicated and encourage them to search for him on other trains besides the two he'd already booked.

He left then, and as much as his ankle was still stabbing with pain and his breathing was labored with the bruising, he took a different street and walked around a full block before approaching Mia's SUV from the opposite direction.

He felt a touch of concern when he saw her sitting perfectly relaxed in the driver's seat. He wondered how long she would have sat there if he'd stuck to his initial plan of boarding the first train out. It also made him wish he'd taken the time to get to know the General, because he was sure Pavić would have worried about her and how she'd cope in the world.

Mia tracked him with her big dark eyes as he approached the car, her expression fathomless. He thought again of Patrice calling her the demon girl. He smiled and she smiled uncertainly back.

After putting his bag on the back seat he got in the front and said, "Okay, that should confuse them for a while. And I have some money, enough to pay for gas and . . ." Eight hundred euros in total—he wasn't sure how long that would last.

"I'm rich."

"That's good, but, you know . . . Okay, that's good, but I have money, in Switzerland. I'll be able to pay back anything you spend on the trip south."

"I don't need it." There was a hint of sadness in her voice that made him uneasy, suggesting that she really did need to help Wes for her own wellbeing as much as for his.

"Do you have a phone I could use, or something linked to the internet?"

"In there, a tablet." She pointed to the glove compartment in front of him.

"Great. I'll look at it once we're on our way."

"And you can read your bible."

He turned and looked at the back seat, then reached over for it, his ribs tightening with pain in response to the movement. Being reunited with it felt like another good reason for his change of plan—after all, the book had saved his life.

"I'm not religious. Patrice gave it to me."

"Patrice is the black man."

"Yeah, the same guy. He gave it to me, so maybe I *will* read it."

"It's good. Shall we go?"

"Sure." He pointed at the console. "Do you need to program in where we're going?"

She laughed, and it was disconcerting for her to be amused by him, she pointed. "It's that way. There will be signs." She started the car, still laughing a little, and drove along to the end of the street.

Wes put the bible aside and reached forward to get the tablet from the glove compartment. He opened Gmail, then entered the account details Raphael had given him, and saw the lone email sitting in his inbox.

And as Wes scrolled through the lists within—names and addresses, cellphone numbers, email addresses—he wondered why

French intelligence hadn't recruited Raphael instead of leaving him locked up with the threat of extradition hanging over him.

Then his eyes snagged on the name Grace Burns. So Grace was in Madrid now, and she and Rachel had been good friends—she had to be the one she'd been visiting. Would Rachel have left her two-and-a-half-year-old son with Grace while she went traveling around southern Spain? Wes was less sure about that.

But Grace would have the answers he needed. She'd know what Rachel's plan had been. She might even have some idea about what had happened to Ethan. Yet even as he contemplated wrapping up the mystery of the boy's whereabouts, he could feel a reluctance creeping in.

If Grace had known, then why had there been no more information about Ethan in the two weeks since the news broke? Were they covering something up? Were the conspiracy sites right—had he been killed in Granada and they didn't want the world to know it for some reason? And in those circumstances, even aside from the fact that Wes was now an active Agency target, would Grace be forthcoming with information?

Would she be forthcoming with Wes anyway? The handful of times they'd met, they hadn't exactly warmed to each other. Grace had always seemed too buttoned-up for Wes's liking, the kind of person whose smile looked more like a wince, who gave off a constant air of aloof disapproval. She'd probably never thought Wes much of a catch for Rachel, and in turn, Wes had never understood how the two women had been friends.

And now Rachel was dead, removing any last reason Grace might have for wanting to help him. So if he went there at all, it couldn't be empty-handed; he had to gather as much information as he could for himself first, information he might use to draw her out.

He spoke aloud as the thought developed, saying, "Actually, I need to go to Granada, not to Madrid."

"Granada, in Andalucía."

"That's correct."

He needed to know if Ethan had been there with her—and if he hadn't, Wes needed to trace Rachel's movements backward to Madrid, to find out where she'd left him.

"It's the same direction."

"You don't mind?" he said. She shook her head. "Thanks. There was an explosion there two weeks ago, a terrorist attack. My ex-wife was killed, and her little boy is missing. I only just found out about him. He's my little boy, too."

She glanced across at him, then back to the road, little more than a mild curiosity as she said, "You're divorced?"

It was strange that she'd fixed on that one small detail, rather than the fact that Rachel was dead and his son was missing.

"Yeah, she divorced me when I got sent to prison."

They were on to busier streets now but she drove with an ease and confidence that seemed at odds with her otherworldly conversational skills.

"Did you get sent to prison for being a soldier?"

"Kind of."

She threw an uneasy glance in his direction, and he got the impression she was thinking she should have asked about this sooner. He'd come bleeding out of the forest after killing three men and he'd been in prison—probably exactly the kind of man a father would warn his daughter about. At least Wes could go some way to reassuring her on that front.

"I worked for the US government, mainly in Turkey, but also Iraq and Syria."

"Against ISIL."

"Mainly. But something went wrong, a helicopter got shot down, with two French aid workers and three civilians on board.

It was kind of an accident, but I was in charge, so I took the blame, and that's why I was in prison."

"Why did people try to kill you today?"

Once again, considering she came across as so guileless, she'd homed in immediately on the crucial fact.

"It's complicated. I think there are people working for my government who no longer trust me to stay quiet. Maybe they think I'll talk about what we were really doing out there, or talk about things they were doing that they shouldn't have been doing."

"You're talking to me about it."

"Not the details. And anyway, they tried to kill me—I don't owe them anything anymore."

"You kill people for the US government and now they want to kill you."

"No. I mean, yes, about them wanting to kill me, but killing other people, that wasn't my job."

"It's why you were in prison. Like a soldier."

"Okay, yeah, kind of. Sometimes I had to kill people, but that wasn't my job. My job was about making the world a safer place."

"My father used to say, sometimes there is no easy way, only the hard way."

"That's true." And to some degree, both Wes and General Pavić had paid for that absence of easy options.

They were out of the city now, driving down the A63 through a mixture of open countryside and villages shielded from the road by high fences. And she was driving fast—not recklessly, but fast all the same.

"Do you have any other family, back in Croatia?"

"No." He thought she might leave it at that, but after thinking about it, she said, "It was just me and my father. Now, just me. I'm taking him back to scatter his ashes. But not yet."

"Of course."

"And what about you, Wes? Do you have any other family?"

Her tone reminded him of someone learning a new language, repeating back the same simple questions they've just been asked, and yet he could tell that her English was pretty much fluent.

"My parents are still alive, and I have two older sisters, some nephews and nieces, but I haven't heard from any of them in three years."

"How do you know they're still alive?"

"I think I'd have heard if they weren't." But now that he'd said it, he wasn't so sure of that. "Truth is, we weren't in touch a lot before—my work made it difficult—but being sent to prison was the final straw. They're respectable people."

"My father was respectable."

Wes nodded, wary of the traps. "I don't doubt it, but I guess I mean a different kind of respectable. My folks were both lawyers, one of my sisters too. The other's a high school principal. I tried to call them after being sentenced, but they'd all changed their numbers."

"They didn't want to hear from you."

He struggled not to laugh—she certainly didn't believe in sugarcoating anything.

"Maybe. Or maybe they were getting calls from the press, stuff like that. I wrote them a letter, telling them it wasn't as bad as it seemed, but I never heard back."

"It's rude if you don't reply to a letter."

"I guess so."

They drove on in silence. For a while, Wes looked out at the countryside, trying to appreciate that this was freedom, after three years of looking at that fence, but he couldn't quite take it in somehow. Everything had the air of a waking dream, and being rescued by Mia only added to the unreality of it all.

He picked up the bible and opened it at the beginning, reading the first page of the creation, familiar even to him. And he read on for a few pages then before seeing something he really hadn't been familiar with.

"How about that? Adam and Eve had more than two children. I never knew that."

"It's an allegory."

"Yeah, I know none of it's true, I just meant—"

"But it's all true. An allegory can still be true. You should read more. The truth is inside the words."

He nodded, wishing Patrice were here, because he and Mia would have found a lot to talk about. But he read on anyway, through pages where the story lost its grip on him. Then he fell asleep, stirring into semi-consciousness now and then, and lulled back into the depths by the comforting noise of the engine and the smooth motion of the car.

# Eleven

When he finally woke properly, the bible was in his lap with his hand resting on top as if he were about to swear an oath. He looked out at the road and the landscape around them, figuring he'd slept as they crossed the border, because this looked like Spain.

He turned and looked at Mia then, relaxed behind the wheel, no less unsettling in appearance, even as he became more used to it.

"Where are we?"

She glanced at him, then back to the road as she pulled out to overtake a truck.

"Close to Segovia."

"Segovia?"

"It's near Madrid. But you don't want to go to Madrid. We'll stay in Segovia tonight. I want to visit the cathedral there."

"Okay, er . . ." He shook himself, stretched in the seat and immediately regretted it, a brutal reminder running through his body of what had happened earlier in the day. "Near Madrid? How long was I asleep?"

He saw the clock on the dash even as she answered. "Seven hours."

"Wow. Have you stopped at all?"

"Yes." She said it as if it should have been obvious. "I booked hotel rooms, in Segovia. I want to visit the cathedral there, in the morning."

"Sure."

Freshly woken, he'd forgotten her strangeness, just as he'd woken many mornings over the past couple of weeks having forgotten that Rachel was dead and that he had a son somewhere out in the world. Those facts had become fully part of him now, and he guessed he'd get used to Mia in time, too.

The hotel she'd booked was an old convent. They went to their rooms after checking in and then met in the restaurant at eight. Mia had changed into a black top of the identical style to the one she'd been wearing earlier.

She offered a polite, slightly formal smile as she sat opposite him, then picked up the menu and studied it intently as if trying to solve a puzzle. He noticed, just inside the sleeve of her top, thin white scars—what looked like the ghosts of long-healed, self-inflicted wounds.

Wes was starving and ordered accordingly. Mia ordered a salad to start and a chicken dish to follow. When the salad arrived she worked at it methodically, joylessly. The plate was almost empty when she put down her knife and fork.

She looked at her wrist, as if suddenly aware that Wes might have seen her scars, and she pulled the sleeve down, almost over her hand.

His instinct was to pretend he hadn't noticed, because really this was nothing to do with him, but unexpectedly she said, "I used to cut myself. And I didn't eat. I made a promise to my father, if he surrendered to the court in The Hague, I would change. Now he's dead."

"But you're still eating."

"Yes. It's important to keep a promise. I wasn't unhappy. I . . ."

"You don't have to explain yourself to me."

"Your name is James Wesley."

The lurch in the conversation threw him momentarily before he caught up. He'd had to give his full name when they were checking in, and he'd wondered whether she'd even noticed and why she hadn't mentioned it. But she had noticed and had stored the fact away until now.

"Yes."

"Why aren't you called James?"

"My family and my wife are the only people who ever called me that. Wes was a nickname from when I was a kid. Even my teachers called me Wes." She looked completely lost somehow. He thought again of how there was something alien about her, like someone stranded in a world for which she wasn't properly equipped. "You know, I appreciate you driving me, Mia, but you can leave any time you like. I can find my own way, if you decide you've had enough. I'd understand."

She stared at him for so long that he thought she might not answer, but it was more that she was decoding what he'd said, as though any ambiguous or implied meanings were slightly beyond her.

Finally, she said, "But I like it. I like to drive. And I have nowhere else, except to scatter my father's ashes."

"You really have no one else back in Croatia?"

"My mother drowned when I was a baby. In the river, with stones in her pockets. I have some aunts and uncles and cousins, but we're not close, not since . . . I have no husband. My father said I'm not the marrying kind, but he said that's fine and I shouldn't worry about it. I don't like to be touched."

That begged a lot of questions, about when it had started or if she'd always been like that; about the reason she was no longer close to her extended family, or if she'd ever been close to them. But it was no business of his, and he guessed she'd tell him if she wanted to.

"Your dad was right, you shouldn't worry about it. We are what we are."

That seemed to please her, and after thinking on it, she said, "Did you know my father?"

"Not really. Clearly my loss."

"He was a good man."

"I heard that."

She didn't finish her main course and didn't have dessert. And though she drank, it amounted to barely a glass of wine across the meal. Wes didn't drink much more himself, finding the alcohol still going too readily to his head—he guessed that would take a while.

Mia went to bed early and the hotel was quiet—so, by eleven, Wes too had gone back to his room. But there was no sleep coming on the back of the six or seven hours he'd had on the journey down.

He turned on the TV and immediately turned it off again, finding the noise obtrusive. That made him think of Rachel—one of the many insignificant things they'd had in common was an aversion to TV in the bedroom.

His thoughts skipped automatically from her to Ethan, even though he knew nothing about him, even though he was nothing more than a name. And because of that, questions rose up to fill the void, questions he couldn't answer and didn't want to think about.

So he sat and read portions of Patrice's bible instead, flicking through and picking pages at random rather than trying to read from the beginning as he had earlier, and drawn in particular to the many lines and passages Patrice had underscored in pencil. And after an hour or so, with tiredness finally creeping up on him, he found one of those lines and turned it over in his mind, moved by its simple invocation.

*Deliver me, O Lord, from the evil man: preserve me from the violent man.*

Some people—his country's enemies—might have viewed him in those terms in the past, and even if his actions hadn't been evil, they had certainly been violent. But now he was the one in need of preservation.

He was probably safe enough for the time being. Mia had granted him an extra layer of cover by driving him, and as much as his former colleagues might expect him to turn up in Granada or Madrid, they wouldn't know exactly where or when. So he was safe for now, but he'd need a greater deliverance than that if he were to have any hope of finding Ethan and filling in those blanks.

# Twelve

Wes was still eating breakfast when Mia came in.

He said, "You want something to eat?"

"I had it already."

"Okay. And you want to go to the cathedral this morning?"

"That's where I've been already."

Now that he looked at her, she had a contented and peaceful air about her that he hadn't noticed before. He imagined that was what the visit to the church had done for her.

"Great. Well, I'm just about finished. Let's get out of here."

"We're going to Granada."

"Yeah." He looked down at the remains of his breakfast then back at Mia, who was still standing behind the chair opposite him. "You been there before?"

"With my father. We visited the Alhambra."

He nodded, wondering if that was what Rachel had been doing there, and whether she'd managed to visit it before being caught up in the attack. She'd always been a bit of a geek for old buildings and historic sites.

Mardin hadn't been particularly notable, not when compared with some of the ancient cities in the region, but in the little under two years she'd spent there, her fascination for its old town had never dimmed. He'd even got to teasing her about it in a good-humored way, because he'd loved that about her, that endless low-key enthusiasm she'd had for the world.

But he didn't want to dwell on thoughts of Rachel, so he stood—with such speed that Mia took a step back—and within twenty minutes they were on their way. They headed south, across the plain around Madrid, through low hills pin-cushioned with neat rows of olive trees, through mountains with white villages tucked in clefts like unmelted snow.

With the same quiet efficiency as the day before, Mia had booked rooms in advance in a *palacio* on the main street. He felt a slight unease when she told him it was the same hotel she'd stayed in with her father, fearing it might bring her grief to the surface, but when they arrived mid-afternoon she showed no signs of it having particular associations for her—it was just a place she'd stayed in before and knew to be okay.

As they were checking in, Wes said to the concierge, "I hope you can help. My ex-wife was one of the victims of the attack the other week, Rachel Richards."

She offered a suitably sympathetic look and said, "The American lady."

"Yeah."

"I'm sorry for your loss, Mr. . . . ." She looked down. "Mr. Wesley."

"Thank you. I wanted to visit the hotel where she was staying. Would you be able to find out which one it was for me?"

"There are lots of hotels in Granada, but of course, I heard from colleagues who had some of the victims as guests. Let me make a few telephone calls while you settle into your rooms."

"Thanks, I'll be back in ten."

As they walked away into the hotel's courtyard, Mia said, "Will I come?"

He wasn't sure what she meant exactly, whether she wanted to come or if she was asking if he expected her to. It felt like an insight, too, into the confusion she probably felt whenever someone made a joke or said something that lacked an explicit meaning.

"You don't have to come, no. But if you want to come, I don't mind. I just need to find out if she had a child with her when she checked in. I'm pretty sure the answer is no, but I want to know if she originally booked for a child."

"So I'll come?"

"Yeah, sure."

"And then I'll visit the cathedral. It's just along the street."

"You like churches, don't you?"

"Yes. I wanted to be a nun when I was small. You can come too."

"No, I'll leave that to you. My wife used to like visiting churches—in fact, any historic building."

"Your *ex*-wife."

"Yeah. Well, if we're gonna be pedantic, my *late* ex-wife."

She stared at him, her eyes shining but still giving away nothing of what was going on within. And then she laughed. He wasn't sure whether she was laughing at him or herself or some random thought, but he couldn't help but laugh, too.

◆ ◆ ◆

Mia was already sitting in reception by the time he got back there. She stood and they approached the desk together.

The concierge smiled and said, "Good news, Mr. Wesley." She reached for a map and for the first time he noticed that she was pregnant. He had missed Rachel's pregnancy—it occurred to him only now, and the realization came with a fleeting and intangible grief. He'd missed so much. All these things that would never be in his grasp again.

63

The concierge opened the map out on the desk and marked a cross on it. "We're here. You can see this is the Albayzín in front of us—the old town—then the Alhambra is across here, and your wife was staying in another nice hotel, the Palacio de Santa Cristina, which is just here." She marked another cross, then drew a line linking them as she said, "It's only a five- or ten-minute walk from here. I told them you might be coming, so they're expecting you."

"Thank you."

"The map is ruined now."

Wes and the concierge both turned to look at Mia, but the concierge smiled and said, "It's fine, it's yours to keep. We have many." She turned back to Wes. "I don't know if you would like to visit the site of the attack, but if you do, it's here in the Albayzín, the Plaza San Martín. I would recommend walking uphill along here, the most famous of the tourist streets, lots of small stores and restaurants, very Moroccan in feel, and then you can cut along the side of the hill to the plaza, or you could walk on to the Mirador de San Nicolás for the view over the Alhambra and come back down to Plaza San Martín."

Wes nodded, taking it all in, not sure if he was the only sane person left. The concierge's odd tour-guide approach to visiting the site where his wife had been murdered a couple of weeks before was, if anything, even weirder than Mia's admittedly flaky comment about the map.

"Thanks, maybe that's something we can look forward to doing in the morning."

His note of sarcasm was lost on the concierge.

"Yes, it's better in the morning, before the crowds and the heat. But you'll visit the hotel now?"

"I think so."

"Good. I told them to expect you."

He thanked her and they left, crossing the busy street outside before cutting through side streets on the way to the last place she'd slept, in the town where she'd died. It hadn't felt real so far, something of a fable clinging to it, or a jarring dream from which he knew he would wake, but there was no doubting he was walking toward reality now.

# Thirteen

The Palacio de Santa Cristina, like their own hotel, was an old building formed around a Moorish courtyard. It was smaller but quietly luxurious, the kind of place he could immediately picture Rachel loving.

As soon as he walked into the reception, a young male concierge stepped forward questioningly. "Mr. Wesley?"

"That's me."

"I'm very sorry for your loss, Mr. Wesley. The manager would like to see you. Perhaps if you would like to take a seat in the courtyard, I'll let her know you're here. Would you like something to drink, some coffee or a cold drink?"

"Coffee would be great, thanks."

The concierge turned to Mia, who responded with alarm, as if she feared he might be about to embrace her. "Madam?"

"Please, some peppermint tea."

The concierge nodded, but now that he'd looked at her he seemed transfixed by her face. Wes had already become used to the otherworldly nature of her appearance, to the extent that it amused him to see other people respond to her as if to a ghostly apparition.

The concierge snapped out of it and said, "I'll be back in a moment. Please, go through and take a seat."

"Before you go." He'd already spun around on his heel but he stopped and faced Wes again, expectant. "Was my wife alone when she was here?"

The concierge offered a sympathetic look and said, "We saw the same stories, but your wife did not have her son with her. He was included in the booking, but she'd left him with friends." The sympathy edged into something else then. "You don't have . . . access?"

Wes knew the whole question of the boy's whereabouts had been hushed up by the authorities, even if he didn't know the reason. The hotel staff and everyone else probably assumed he'd been found and was safe with relatives, or with his father, and there was only one way Wes could answer without arousing suspicion.

"He wasn't my son."

"Ah. I see." The concierge gestured toward the courtyard. "Please, take a seat, and the manager will be with you shortly."

They walked through and, once they were sitting, Mia said, "What's his name?"

"Who?"

"The boy who's missing."

It was the first time she'd expressed any real interest in Wes's reasons for being here.

"Oh, Ethan. Ethan Richards."

"Not Wesley."

"No."

"Because he's not your son."

"No, I just said that to the concierge. I'm pretty sure he's mine. That's why I'm here—I need to find out where he is, make sure he's okay."

"That's what fathers do."

"I guess so," he said, even as he knew he'd never be much more of a father than that unless the Agency had a change of heart. And he didn't want to think that far ahead anyway—one problem at a time.

They sat in the small ornately tiled courtyard with water playing gently in the fountain at its center. He could easily imagine Rachel emerging from one of the doors, crossing the courtyard but getting sidetracked, looking up mesmerized by the galleried landings above. He thought he'd successfully put away all his memories and feelings for her, but it was painful to think of her now, to think of never seeing her again in that private little reverie of hers.

Someone did emerge from a door across the way, but it was a waitress, bringing their drinks. Then a few minutes later a smartly dressed middle-aged woman came out of the same door on the other side of the courtyard. She was carrying a large padded envelope and smiling as she approached.

"Mr. Wesley, I'm pleased to meet you, but sorry it's in such terrible circumstances." Wes stood and she said, "Please, don't get up. I'm Beatriz Fuentes, the hotel manager."

They shook hands, the manager glancing down at his bandages, and then Wes said, "This is Mia."

Wes was relieved when, instead of leaning over the table to shake her hand, the manager simply nodded with a smile and said, "Pleased to meet you, Mia."

"Hello."

Beatriz sat, placing the envelope on the seat next to her.

"I understand you and Miss Richards were divorced?"

"That's correct."

She looked at him with what appeared to be understanding, but her expression also suggested she knew more about him than his marital status—a couple of the recent news reports had mentioned him by name, or rather had described Rachel as "the former wife of the disgraced CIA officer James Wesley."

"I was part of a US operation that went wrong, and my negligence resulted in people dying. I was sent to prison—we both felt it would be better for Rachel if, well, you know . . ."

It was a lie expertly interwoven with strands of the truth, and Rachel would have laughed to see him construct it, but Beatriz looked touched in response.

"A sad situation." She looked at Mia, maybe wondering how she fitted into the equation, but when Mia openly stared back at her, Beatriz seemed unnerved and turned quickly to Wes. "Some people came for your wife's things, people from the US embassy in Madrid. They told us that the next of kin is the brother, and that they would send the things to him."

"Technically that's true."

She appeared not to hear him, her mind on another track. "This was an oversight. If they had asked for the contents of the room safe, of course, we would have looked, but we didn't think to check until after they'd left. It was an upsetting time, for all of us, for everyone in the city."

Wes glanced at the envelope. "There was something in the safe? Her passport?"

"No, and perhaps that's why they didn't ask—the passport was with her when she died. I tried to contact the people, but the number they left . . ." She shook her head, baffled.

Wes could imagine someone from the Madrid station being sent down here to collect Rachel's belongings, resenting it, feeling it was a mundane task beneath their pay grade, giving the hotel manager a false number rather than risk having her call every ten minutes with something else she'd remembered.

"Perhaps under the circumstances, it's more appropriate for you to have them anyway, as a keepsake."

She picked up the envelope and handed it to him. It felt fat and heavy. He opened it and looked inside without taking out any of the contents. He could see paperwork, receipts, tickets.

Resting it on his lap, he said, "Thank you. Do you know when she planned to check out?"

"The day after the attack, I believe. The concierge told me she'd arranged a car to take her to Málaga, but she wasn't staying there, only visiting the Picasso Museum. She planned to take the train from Málaga to Seville."

"So the car was taking her to the Picasso Museum?"

"No, to the railway station."

"Did she say why?"

"No, but maybe she wanted to buy her ticket first, check the times. I don't know."

Those were things she would have done online, and something about this diversion sounded wrong. It sounded to Wes like she'd been covering her tracks, and that made him wonder if it had actually been a working trip. That would explain her not wanting the child with her, but according to her brother she'd left the Agency six months earlier, so maybe she'd been freelancing, or Adam was wrong.

Whatever the case, she hadn't wanted the driver to know where she was really going in Málaga. So there was little point in Wes going there either, because without that information, he wouldn't know what to look for or where to start.

Besides, Wes's job was to work out where she'd been, not where she'd been going. He had to concentrate on moving backward through her final days until he found Ethan.

He looked across at the fountain, once again imagining her standing there. "I bet she loved this hotel."

"I didn't meet her myself. She was here such a short time before it happened, but the staff who met her said she appeared very happy here. I think you can take comfort in that."

Rachel had felt like a stranger to him these last few years. Even when Dupont had broken the news of her death, it had seemed like news of a life far removed from his own. Yet now, little by little, he could feel her coming back to him, and he already knew with certainty that she wouldn't have been happy—she'd had a son, something she'd wanted so much, and for whatever reason, she'd been without him here. She might well have been taking pleasure from the beauty of this place, but no, happiness would never have come into it.

# Fourteen

They walked back, but parted en route, with Mia taking a pilgrim's detour to the cathedral and Wes heading back to the hotel. He made his way into the courtyard when he got there, sitting at a table in the cloister. There were a few other people sitting at tables here and there in the shade, but the atmosphere was hushed.

A waiter in a white tunic came gliding along the cloister and Wes ordered a cold drink before carefully emptying out the contents of the envelope onto the table. He thought of placing something on top of the various pieces of paper to hold them down, but there was no need—there wasn't even a hint of a breeze, the stillness almost oppressive.

Once it was all before him, he picked up a stack of receipts and looked idly through them. There were credit card receipts from restaurants and cafés, train tickets, two hotel receipts, both from Seville.

He opened the two hotel receipts next to each other on the table. She'd stayed in one for three days, then another for two days. Why would she move? In both cases, the second sheet with the detailed breakdown had been removed and discarded, the marks from the staples the only sign that they'd ever been there, so there was nothing to show whether she'd been in both hotels alone.

He folded them, then looked at the train tickets and felt a sudden giddy rush in his blood. A ticket from Madrid to Seville, for one adult and one child under the age of four. Ethan had been in Seville with her, which meant she hadn't left him with Grace in Madrid. And she had meant to go back to Seville via Málaga, which meant he could still be there now, a couple of hours away from where Wes was sitting. She'd left him with friends, that's what everyone kept saying, and maybe those friends were in Seville.

He looked back through the sheets of paper and found a pre-booked printed ticket from Málaga to Seville. Then he found a cash receipt for Renfe, the train company, for just under two hundred euros, but couldn't find the corresponding ticket to go with it.

Mia walked into the courtyard and Wes waved to her and she came over, exuding the same air of peace he'd noticed after her visit to the cathedral in Segovia.

But when she sat down she said, "It was for tourists, not for prayer. I couldn't even light a real candle."

"That's too bad. Maybe Seville will be better."

Her eyes brightened. "You need to go to Seville?"

"I think so, in the morning, if that's okay."

"But I thought, in the morning, you wanted to visit the place where your ex-wife died."

"I don't really need to see it. I'm not sure I even want to."

"But I think you should. It's important." He was taken aback by her certainty, but before he could say anything, she added, "We could go now—it's still light, and too early for dinner. Then we could leave for Seville after breakfast. It's a good plan, I think."

"Okay."

He started to put everything back into the envelope, and it seemed only now that she noticed it all.

"There are lots of postcards."

"Yeah, she liked to buy them, write on them. She never sent them." He picked one up and handed it to her, but she refused to take it.

"It's not for me."

"It's not for anyone. She'd just write down random things." He turned the card over and looked at the back. "This one's from Seville. She says there's the most beautiful scent all over the city, and she should find out what it is."

"Oh." Mia seemed to weigh up what she thought of this idiosyncrasy of Rachel's, then said brightly, "So, shall we go, to the place where she died?"

"Sure."

He took the envelope back to his room and then they set off, following the tourist route the concierge had suggested. They climbed a steep narrow street hemmed in by small Arabic stores and restaurants, the owners of the former trying to attract Mia with their scarves or various decorative objects, the owners of the latter asking Wes if he liked good Moroccan food.

There were swarms of day-trippers, but also plenty of people lounging or drifting about who looked more permanent in some disheveled way—immigrants, washed-up hippies, an African man who walked down the street toward them shaving himself absent-mindedly with a disposable razor.

Wes and Mia climbed higher, beyond the tightly packed stores, but Wes could feel his ankle twinging with the strain of the ascent so they turned off, moving sideways around the hill of the Albayzín where they found quieter streets. There were still pockets of tourists even here, trudging wearily through the late-afternoon heat. A decent number of them were staring at the maps on their phones, trying to work out where they'd gone astray.

Wes and Mia also got lost and he pulled the map from his pocket, looking at the route the concierge had marked. They weren't far off, and after a couple more turns through tight white-washed streets, they stepped into the Plaza San Martín and the site of the attack.

The café where it had happened was closed, a couple of work-men just tidying up for the day, but the signs of rebuilding suggested either the explosion had been massive or that the owners had simply taken the opportunity to remodel. Another café was open on the opposite side of the almost empty square—a handful of tables, only one of them occupied.

"Shall we stay for a drink?"

Mia looked at him as if he'd made a lame joke. "But it's closed."

"No, not here—I mean the café across the square."

"Oh. Yes."

They strolled across and took seats. There were a couple of empty tables between them and the only other customer, an old man who sat leaning on his walking stick.

A waiter came out a moment later, and before he'd even had a chance to greet them, Mia said, "A white wine, please."

"Of course." He looked bemused. "Sir?"

"*Hola*. Er, I guess I'll have a glass of red, thanks." The waiter nodded, but before he could disappear, Wes said, "I guess you've been quieter since the attack?"

"You guess wrong." Wes noticed he had a slight American accent, suggesting he'd spent time there. "This square's normally pretty quiet. But now, we get a lot of people coming just to see it. Curious, you know. People like you."

"His ex-wife was killed there. With a bomb."

Mia pointed for good measure, and yet Wes already knew her well enough to know she wasn't trying to make the waiter feel bad or put him in his place; she was just stating a fact.

But there was no question the waiter felt bad anyway.

"Man, I'm sorry, I didn't—"

"Don't worry about it. I know you didn't mean anything by it."

"I'm sorry anyway. I'll get your drinks."

They sat in silence. Mia was staring intently at the partly restored café across the square from them. He couldn't detect any sign of emotion or even curiosity in those unfathomable eyes, but she stared all the same. In the end, Wes turned and looked himself, and sure enough, a few people strolled into the square and stood there, pointing at the attack site before moving on.

The waiter came out carrying a tray and put down the two glasses of wine and some olives in a bowl. He spoke a few words in Spanish to the old man as he walked back inside but received no response that was audible.

Wes wanted to know where his son was—that was the only reason he was here. It was true, a part of him was also curious about what it was that Rachel might have been doing on this leg of her trip, what it was that had made her decide it might be better to leave Ethan with someone else.

Until now, though, the attack itself hadn't interested him—it was just the random way in which Rachel had happened to die too soon, a piece of bad luck no different to an air crash or cancer or any number of other causes. Despite all the conspiracy theories, in Wes's experience terrorism was rarely that interesting.

Even sitting here in this square, it was of only incidental interest, and yet . . . For the first time, his thoughts engaged with the event itself, engaged in a way that reminded him of the way he used to think, before three years of prison dulled his mind.

Thinking aloud, he said, "This is a strange place for a suicide bomber to attack. Why here?"

He was aware of Mia turning to look at him, and he turned too and met her gaze.

"Terrorists attack where you least expect—that's what my father told me."

Wes felt a warmth for the late General Pavić, imagining him trying to impart all these pieces of advice to his daughter, ways of surviving in a hostile world.

"Your father was right, but there's still some logic." Even as he spoke, the ways in which there was an absence of logic in this attack began to pile up on top of each other. "Ignore the fact that this city has a sizable Muslim population. Let's say one of them becomes radicalized and decides to detonate a bomb and kill as many tourists as possible. Where are the busiest places in Granada?"

"The cathedral was busy, and I remember when I went to the Alhambra with my father, there were so many people."

"Exactly. Or the Mirador place the concierge mentioned with the view over the Alhambra. Any one of those places would have been perfect. Why a sleepy square with hardly any people in it?"

She took out her phone and looked at it for a minute in silence. Wes sipped at his wine—it was too warm, and he wished now he'd gone for white like Mia.

"The attacker was called Hassan Berrada. He was a Muslim, from Seville."

"So why didn't he blow up some tourist site in Seville? Why come all this way?"

She read on intently, then said, "They think he planned to detonate the bomb at the Alhambra, but it went off early."

"Does it say anything else about him?"

"They think he was radicalized online, but they also say he had mental health problems."

That made Wes suspicious. On the one hand, there was a better than average chance that someone carrying out a terrorist attack had mental health problems. But he also knew it was the kind of sweeping statement used all the time by the authorities, usually as a way of defending their failure to preempt an attack, knowing full well it was almost impossible to disprove.

But he knew he was falling into the same trap that the conspiracy theorists fell into in the aftermath of terrorist attacks—that of looking for meaning where there was none. Maybe there were things about this that seemed odd, but nothing odd enough to distract Wes from the more important matters he had to focus on.

The reasons a young man had chosen to blow himself up in a quiet Spanish square, even if they could be fully deduced and explained, would serve no purpose to the bereaved, and certainly not to the victims. Hassan Berrada had nothing to tell Wes other than what he already knew, that Rachel was dead and that there would be no more chapters written between them.

# Fifteen

They set off early the next morning, a low mist clinging to the hills around Granada, clearing only as they descended onto the plain. Mia hadn't been to Seville before and was excited about seeing it, apparently oblivious to how strange the circumstances were.

She'd booked a hotel before breakfast, and that was the other side of this woman. It had struck Wes a few times that she often referred to pieces of advice her father had given her, and he could imagine the old man trying to protect and guide her, knowing that she was ill-equipped for the world. Yet she was unfazed by practicalities like hotel bookings or driving—he hadn't seen her use the satnav once.

And when they got to Seville and drove into the old town, she navigated the tight and twisting streets with ease, even as others edged nervously between the confining walls of buildings. It was as if she'd calculated how big the SUV was, worked out that it fit in the gap available, and was completely confident as a result.

The hotel was right next to the cathedral, so once they'd checked in, Wes said, "I guess you'll want to go light a candle?"

"Not yet. It's not a good time."

The concierge nodded agreement as though he were part of the conversation. "It's very busy at this time of day. Early or late is best."

Wes turned to look at him and said, "I need to get to a hotel, the Alfonso XIII."

"Sure, I can show you on the map."

Without meaning to, Wes threw a glance at Mia, then faced the concierge again. "No need. Just point me in the general direction."

"Okay. If you go around the cathedral on the right-hand side, then keep going straight ahead, you can't really miss it. You'll see signs."

Mia stared at the concierge, fixing him with those dark eyes, and Wes found himself holding his breath, wondering what she might be about to say, but then she smiled and said, "I like this hotel."

"Thank you."

A short while later they set off into the deadening heat of early afternoon, keeping to the shade and out of the crowds wherever they could. Mia hardly looked at the cathedral as they passed, but she stared with alarm and confusion at the line of people waiting to gain entry.

Wes thought of Ethan and how close to him he might be right now. There were plenty of people walking about the place with small children and he found that oddly unnerving. He'd still not even seen a picture so he could have easily walked past his own son without knowing it. And then he thought of Ethan pining for his mother, too young to understand that she wasn't coming back, and Wes didn't want to think about that.

He welcomed the distraction when Mia said, "It's orange blossom."

"Excuse me?" He looked at her, just to be sure she'd been talking to him.

She pointed at the tree nearest them. "In the postcard, your ex-wife wanted to find out about the scent. It's orange blossom."

Wes noticed it now, a sweet delicate fragrance hanging in the air, and he imagined Rachel wandering around these streets. Had she ever found out what the scent was? And where had she been and what had she seen while she was here? He was increasingly certain this hadn't been entirely a vacation for Rachel, but even so, she had experienced these streets, savored this orange blossom scent, just as he was doing now.

"Why did your ex-wife leave you?"

"Like I told you, I was sent to prison."

"But you were a soldier. You didn't do anything wrong."

"True. It's kind of complicated." He looked across at her to see if that was enough, but he could see she was waiting for more and there was no reason not to tell her—even if he still owed any loyalty to the Agency, most of his fall was in the public domain anyway. "Look, there was a person we were targeting, someone who was causing problems. We got the details of the flightpath for his helicopter and we brought it down. But it was the wrong helicopter, and the aid workers killed were from an agency which had accused the CIA of carrying out crimes in the region. The three civilians were a couple of journalists and a UN observer looking into those claims. So it looked bad on us. We admitted friendly fire, promised to punish those responsible, and I fell on my sword."

"That's just an expression."

"Yes."

"So your ex-wife, she thought you did a bad thing."

"She works for the government too, so she knew what we were doing. In fact, I think I was the one who suggested she leave, to protect her own career."

Even as he said it he knew that was a lie, one he'd told himself numerous times. It was near the end of that weeklong escape— a week in which he now knew he might well have fathered a child—that he'd told her she needed to distance herself from him, for the sake of her career. "I've been thinking about that," she'd said. "I was thinking a quick divorce would be best, and once you're out, well, we can see how things are." He'd been stung and admiring in some way and maybe even relieved—as happy as they'd been in that week, as easy and comfortable with each other, that one sentence told him all he needed to know, that she no longer loved him, and he was pleased because that would make it easier for her, for both of them.

"She left you because you went to prison, and they let you out of prison because she died."

"Yeah . . . Crazy, huh?"

"Yes. I think it's a difficult life to be a soldier." She smiled sadly, and he knew she wasn't thinking about him now.

The concierge hadn't been kidding about being unable to miss the Alfonso XIII. It was a landmark building in a prime location, even in a city full of landmark buildings in prime locations. They walked through the gates, up the short sweep of the driveway, and climbed the steps to the main lobby.

Wes stopped as soon as they got inside. It was busy, people milling around or waiting to speak to one of the half dozen staff who were already dealing with other guests. Beyond the lobby Wes could see the internal Moorish courtyard, which was equally busy, with most of the tables occupied.

Mia stopped and turned, smiling at him. "Why did you stop walking? I was talking to you."

"Sorry, I just . . . This isn't the kind of hotel Rachel would've stayed in."

It was too big, too bustling, a great place in its own way, but just not what Rachel would have booked.

"But she did stay here."

Wes nodded, because that was the mystery. Rachel had booked into a place that wouldn't have suited her at all, and had stayed for three days. Why, and what had she been doing during that time? And at what point during her stay in this city had she said goodbye to her son, and could she have imagined that she would never see him again?

# Sixteen

Despite the melee of people coming and going, they managed to attract the attention of one of the concierges within a few minutes and asked to speak to a manager. As soon as Wes mentioned Rachel's name the concierge became animated, as if they'd been waiting for someone to come and ask about her. He showed Wes and Mia into a small conference room with eight chairs around a dark wooden table and asked them to wait.

Mia looked around the room and then sat at the head of the table, facing the door. It was the chair Wes would have chosen for himself and he hovered for a moment before choosing one of the others.

No sooner had he settled than the door opened and a suited man bustled into the room. He was probably under forty, tanned and healthy-looking, but his hair was completely gray.

He put a hand out and said, "Mr. Richards, I'm Carlos, the deputy manager."

"Mr. Wesley. Rachel kept her maiden name after we were married."

"I'm sorry, my mistake."

They shook hands. Wes had removed the bandages that morning and found the cuts were healing well, and it felt good now to be unencumbered. Carlos turned to Mia, his hand still outstretched.

"This is Mia. She doesn't like to be touched."

"Of course," said Carlos, as if it were the most natural thing in the world. He withdrew his hand and gave a deferential nod. "Welcome, both, and Mr. Webley . . ."

"Wesley."

"My apologies. Mr. Wesley, I'm sorry for your loss."

"Thanks, I appreciate it."

Carlos walked around the table and sat facing Wes, then said, "Might I get you something to eat or drink?"

"No, thank you, we won't take up too much of your time. I'm sure you've heard that our son is missing." Carlos nodded gravely, and something in his expression suggested to Wes that he'd spoken about this more than once, maybe to the Spanish police, certainly to the Americans. "I'm just retracing Rachel and Ethan's movements, so I wanted to check that Ethan was still with her when she was staying with you."

"Yes. They stayed with us for three nights. Actually, I spoke with her myself when she arrived, and she asked me about the boats for hire in the Plaza de España—she said the little boy loved boats."

"Ethan was with her when she spoke to you?"

"Of course. A sweet little boy."

"Did you see her again at all?"

Carlos shrugged as though Wes were asking him something impossible. "You know, it's a large hotel, many guests, and . . ."

"No, I understand." It *was* a large hotel, with many guests, and as he'd already figured, not the kind of place that Rachel would have booked ordinarily. Wes felt the stirrings of a deeper understanding, a lead promising enough that he felt nervous about pursuing it. "Would it be possible to speak to the housekeeper who looked after their room?"

"Er . . ." The expression suggested Wes had asked another impossible question, but then Carlos appeared to relent and offered a sympathetic smile. "Let me see what I can do. I'll be back very shortly."

"Thank you."

Carlos left and they sat in silence for a while before Mia said, "Why do you want to speak to the housekeeper?"

"Just a hunch."

"Hunch? What is hunch?"

"Like an idea. You know when you're reading a mystery novel and you have an idea who the murderer might be but you're not sure why? That's a hunch."

She smiled. "Hunch." She looked on the verge of laughing. "Hunch."

"Hunch," said Wes, smiling too, warmed by the simple joy she was taking from this new word.

"You want to speak to the housekeeper because you have a hunch that your ex-wife didn't stay here."

Wes's smile fell away, and he was curious now. "How did you know?"

"I had a hunch too." She laughed a little. "Because you said she wouldn't stay somewhere like this. And it's so busy. It would be easy to pretend."

"That's more or less it. And she made a point of being remembered, speaking to Carlos about boats—that isn't like her either."

Wes turned toward the door because he could hear Carlos approaching, talking rapidly in Spanish. Then the door opened and he came in with a young dark-haired woman trailing behind him in a housekeeper's uniform. Wes stood.

"We're in luck," said Carlos. "This is Inés, Mr. Wesley. She was the housekeeper for your wife and son's room during their stay."

"Hello, Inés." He shook her hand but she looked uncomfortable, and even more so as he said, "Thanks for coming to speak to us."

"Inés doesn't speak English." Carlos translated for her and she smiled now and nodded at Wes and at Mia. "What would you like to ask her?"

They didn't seem inclined to sit, so Wes remained standing too, and was conscious of Mia sitting at the head of the table as if watching a performance.

"I know it was a few weeks back now but I wonder if she met my wife, my son, if she remembers anything about their stay."

Carlos nodded and then spoke to Inés. An exchange followed between them, a rapid to-and-fro, with certainty from her and growing confusion from him.

Eventually Carlos turned back to Wes. "I don't understand. Inés doesn't think they ever stayed in the room. The suitcase was there, unopened, the beds were never slept in." Inés was staring at Carlos as he spoke, then interjected and there was another brief exchange before Carlos looked helplessly at Wes. "She said the cellphone was also left in the room, on charge."

"I understand."

"You do?" Carlos spoke once more to Inés, a simple question this time, met with a simple answer that caused him to sigh.

"What did you just ask?"

"I asked why she'd never mentioned this before."

"And?"

"She said no one ever asked her before." Inés shook her head in acknowledgment, suggesting she had a little English. Then Carlos said, "You don't seem surprised, Mr. Wesley."

"Well, I know my wife, I guess. But I'm sure you'll understand that I can't go into any more detail."

Carlos nodded, though it was apparent he didn't understand at all. Why would someone pay for three nights in a luxury hotel and use it as little more than a left-luggage facility? And where would someone go for three days without their cellphone? Wes didn't have the answers to those questions, but at least he knew the questions, and he knew also that somewhere behind them lay the key to Ethan's whereabouts.

And wherever that was, he could pretty much guarantee it wasn't Seville. He was equally certain the second hotel would confirm his suspicions, that Rachel had used the three days to take Ethan far away from there, and that he hadn't been with her when she'd returned.

There was something else, too. She couldn't have known she'd get caught up in a terrorist attack, but the lengths she'd gone to in concealing her movements beforehand suggested she'd been involved in something high-risk. He'd long learned that even if life was full of coincidences, those coincidences sometimes needed to be investigated. And maybe this was one of those times.

At the very least, if Rachel had been involved in something sensitive, other people would be looking for links, too. So he'd have to visit the family of Hassan Berrada after all, to find out which Americans had also visited in the weeks since the attack, and to find out what questions they'd asked.

# Seventeen

The Corral del Rey wasn't far from the Alfonso XIII, but Wes felt a growing sense of urgency now and asked one of the bellhops to flag a taxi for them.

Once they were on their way, Wes said, "Mia, could you look on your phone to see if you can find an address for Hassan Berrada?"

She looked at him with a mix of confusion and concern, and he was half expecting her to remind him that Berrada had blown himself up in Granada. But before she could reply, the driver cleared his throat and caught Wes's eye in the rearview.

"Berrada? The terrorist?"

"Yeah."

"I can take you there. I take a journalist there last week or the week before."

"Okay. I want to go to Corral del Rey first."

"Sure, Hotel Corral del Rey, then to the apartment Berrada."

"Thanks. Is it . . . an immigrant neighborhood?"

The driver frowned, and at first Wes thought he hadn't understood the question but then he said, "No, no. In Seville, no. We have not many Moroccan families and they all, er . . ." He took both hands off the wheel and waved them about.

"Integrate?"

"Yes, yes. I take you there, after Corral del Rey."

Wes sensed Mia's gaze on him and when he turned to face her she said, "Why do you want to go there?"

"I'm convinced my wife wasn't really on vacation. I think she was working. It's a long shot, but I want to ask the Berrada family about any American visitors they might have had since the attack. It might help me understand what Rachel was doing, and that might help me understand where she left Ethan." He heard his own words as an objective observer might, and could feel his heart sinking in response. "I know, it seems unlikely, but the key in our line of work is exploring every angle."

"You don't want them to say sorry?"

"The family? No. It's not their fault. Their son died too."

The driver had turned into narrower streets as they'd talked, and Mia pointed now and said, "There it is. Corral del Rey."

Wes nodded. It was much smaller than the hotel they'd just been in, less conspicuous, and he could see already it was much more Rachel's style.

They paid the driver and Wes said, "Five minutes, okay?"

The driver looked at his watch but glanced around too. "The street is very narrow. If another car comes . . ."

"If another car comes, sound the horn and we'll come back."

He nodded and Wes and Mia headed into the calm interior. A woman with long mousy hair was walking across the small foyer but she turned and smiled at them as they walked in and greeted them in Spanish.

"Hello. My wife stayed here a few weeks back—Rachel Richards."

The woman's smile broke down and she put a hand over her heart. "I'm very sorry for what happened. Would you like—"

"No, I'm sorry, we have a car waiting." Even as he spoke, his eyes were being drawn to the interior of the hotel, and he wanted to stay and get the feel of it and ask about Rachel's time here, to imagine her in this space. "I just need to ask one thing. Was her son with her?"

"No, he wasn't. He was meant to come, but she told us he was staying with friends instead. We told this to the person from the American embassy."

"Did the person from the embassy leave a card or a contact number?"

"I don't think so. I could ask, but I don't think so."

"No, it's fine. Thanks for your time."

"You're welcome. If there's anything else we can do . . ." Her words dried up, acknowledging the obvious truth, that there was nothing any of them could do, or almost nothing.

They walked back out. The driver hadn't sounded his horn, and he looked relaxed sitting there, despite the fact that a small truck and another taxi were now waiting behind him, both drivers looking oddly resigned.

They got into the car and he waved to the vehicles behind and said, "So, Berrada apartment."

They started to crawl along the narrow street, squeezing past pedestrians, and Mia said, "Three days is a long time."

Wes looked at her and smiled. Three days *was* a long time, and Rachel couldn't have flown but she still could have reached anywhere in Spain or Portugal or even most of France in a day and a half. It didn't help solve the mystery of her actions, but it pretty much confirmed once and for all that Ethan most likely wasn't in Seville, and that meant they didn't need to be here either.

# Eighteen

It was a fifteen-minute drive to the neighborhood where the Berradas lived, a mainly residential area of neat modern apartment buildings on tree-lined streets. The driver pulled up outside one of the buildings and pointed.

"Apartment Four. You want I wait?"

"No, we'll make our own way back." Wes paid him and they got out of the car.

The street was almost eerily quiet, the peacefulness made more striking by traffic passing through the next intersection, which the departing taxi was already approaching. The street door to the building was ajar so they pushed through it and took the stairs.

There was no noise within the building either, and when Wes rang the bell there was no sound from inside the Berrada apartment. He was just about to state the obvious, that they might have gone away, when the door opened and a young man stood facing them.

He was slim, dark-haired. He also had a black eye. He said something wearily in Spanish.

Wes said, "I don't understand, I'm sorry."

"You're American? Journalists or . . ."

He didn't finish, but Wes guessed he meant "government," and that offered a little more hope that there had already been representatives from the government here.

"Neither. My name's James Wesley. My wife was one of the people killed. Rachel Richards."

The young man stared at him, the look of someone who wished he could disappear and not be part of the situation he found himself in.

Wes added quickly, "I haven't come here to cause trouble . . ."

"Then why *have* you come?"

"I was hoping . . . I just, I had a couple questions, but . . ." He looked at the kid in front of him who was struggling so hard to keep his composure, and as much as Wes wanted those answers, he knew he shouldn't have come here. "I'm sorry. Look, I shouldn't have disturbed you."

"But you did." There seemed a hint of a challenge in the young man's voice and in his expression, but it lasted only a moment before he stepped back, opening the door wider by way of invitation. "Please, come in." Wes hesitated, surprised by the apparent change of tone and unsure what had brought it about. "I am Hamdi Berrada. Hassan was my brother."

"Okay, thanks. This is my friend Mia."

They nodded to each other as Wes and Mia stepped into the apartment and Hamdi closed the door behind them.

"Please, this way." He led them into a large living room decorated in the Moroccan style, with low couches lining the walls. He was speaking softly in Arabic even as he entered the room and Wes took in the people sitting there—his parents; a girl of about fourteen; a boy a little younger still; a very elderly woman; another woman who might have been Hamdi's older sister, a sleeping baby in her arms.

The parents in particular looked broken and old beyond their years, but everyone in the room looked bereft, a mixture of loss and confusion on their faces. As Hamdi spoke, something in his words caused the woman with the baby to gasp, and Wes guessed he'd just reached the point of telling his family who these visitors were.

Wes looked at the parents and said, "Thank you for allowing me to come into your home. I'm sorry for your loss."

Hamdi translated and Mr. Berrada looked in danger of breaking down in response. Instead, he stood and gestured for the two of them to sit. As they took their places, the younger woman handed the baby to the elderly lady, then left the room, together with the girl.

Mrs. Berrada barely seemed present, but Mr. Berrada spoke a few words. His son looked impatient, even angry, in response, but then his father nodded with finality and Hamdi sighed before translating.

"My father thanks you for coming, despite the shame on this house, and begs your forgiveness."

"There's nothing to forgive, Mr. Berrada. You lost a son."

Mr. Berrada responded with a look of gratitude and reached out to take his wife's hand. Wes turned his attention to Hamdi.

"I'm sorry to get right to the point of my visit. I'm sure you've had visitors from the American embassy or the consulate here in Seville, and I just wondered . . ."

He stopped because Hamdi was shaking his head.

He sounded bitter and bemused as he said, "But we haven't, Mr. Wesley. Not one. It's strange, is it not? My brother was radicalized, so we might expect many people from your government, but none, not after the attack."

"I see." And then Wes caught up with the words. "Not *after* the attack? You mean . . . ?"

Hamdi looked across at his parents, then stood and left the room. Wes could hear low voices elsewhere in the apartment, while all was stillness here, like people awaiting a train that wouldn't arrive.

Hamdi came back in and said, "My sisters are making tea, but perhaps we could take a walk, you and I?"

"Sure." Wes stood and turned to Mia. "Would you like to come, or wait?"

She smiled. "I like it here."

He smiled back, despite the situation, and nodded to her, then walked out into the hallway, following Hamdi. But the young man stopped at the door before he left, turning to Wes, fixing him with a fierce and urgent stare.

"My brother was not a terrorist, Mr. Wesley."

It was something Wes had heard many times before. No one ever wanted to think that their brother, their son, sometimes their daughter, had become so disillusioned or so driven by hate that they'd been willing to kill themselves and countless others in the pursuit of some delusional objective.

Looking at the bruised and earnest face of Hamdi Berrada, it was almost tempting to believe he was the exception, that his brother had been framed or tricked by persons unknown. But he was wrong, probably, and Hassan Berrada had been exactly what he'd seemed, an angry and pliable young man, easily indoctrinated into carrying out mass murder.

"I believe you," said Wes, with such conviction that Hamdi appeared satisfied, and they walked out and down onto the street.

# Nineteen

Once they were walking, Wes said, "So, tell me about your brother."

"Hassan was simple, everybody knew it. He was so sweet-natured, but frustrating too, because he was so gullible. Moon landings, Roswell, all kinds of strange conspiracies he believed without a moment of doubt. But most of all, he wanted to be a spy. James Bond. He loved James Bond. And he was talking about it more than ever in the weeks before the attack."

"So you don't believe he was radicalized."

"Of course not. We are a moderate family. My parents chose to come to Seville because they wanted to become part of Spanish society. And Hassan also loved America and American culture—he was so excited about being able to come and visit me there." He noticed a glance from Wes and nodded in response. "I was planning to go to MIT next year, a grad program in electrical engineering and computer science. What chance do I have of doing that now?"

"How did you get the black eye?"

He smiled, an edge of bitterness. "A misunderstanding."

"What did you mean when you talked about Americans visiting before the attack?"

Hamdi frowned, looking uncertain now. "I don't know for sure that he was American. I never spoke to him. I saw him a few times talking to Hassan, firing him up with something." Wes's heart sank, seeing that this might just be a case of a young man desperate to exonerate his brother and rescue his memory. "He looked American."

"What does an American look like?"

Hamdi shook his head, frustrated. "I don't know, I mean . . . he *looked* American, and once or twice, Hassan slipped up and said it would be different when he was in the CIA, then everyone would know they'd underestimated him."

Wes let out a sigh, realizing too late how that sigh sounded, as if he felt his time was being wasted here, which was actually what he did feel. "So you think an American recruited your brother with promises of being in the CIA, and then presumably you think they gave him a mission to deliver a backpack to Granada, and because he was gullible he never would have suspected what was in the pack or that he was being set up to be a suicide bomber, to blow up a handful of random people in a random café. And all of that because . . . ?"

Even as he said it, Wes acknowledged in his own mind that one of those random people had been a former intelligence analyst with the CIA, who might well have been working freelance at the time. It was as beguiling a thought in its own way as Hamdi's belief that his brother had been duped rather than radicalized.

"I know how it sounds, Mr. Wesley. But please, go back to my original point and consider it. If my brother was radicalized, that suggests somebody radicalized him, online or in person, so why has no one from your government visited or called us at all in these recent weeks? And I'll tell you another thing—"

Wes spotted a sudden movement as something flew towards them. Instinctively, he snatched it out of the air a couple of feet short of it hitting Hamdi. It was an apricot, but hard and unripe enough that it would have hurt, or maybe even wounded him—the impact had left the freshly healed wounds on Wes's hand smarting.

Wes spun around and spotted a couple of teenagers standing behind the partial cover of a tree on the other side of the street. One of them shouted something and the other laughed in response. It sounded abusive, threatening. Wes also had to admit, from where they were standing it had either been a pretty good throw or a lucky one.

He turned to Hamdi. "You want me to have a word with them?"

To his surprise, Hamdi looked back with barely concealed contempt. "*A word?* And what about tomorrow, and the day after? What good will your word do then? Our life here is over."

Wes stared across at them anyway, and something about his gaze persuaded the two young punks to walk on. Wes watched them slouch away, but despite Hamdi's protestations he couldn't resist one small lesson at least. He threw the apricot, hard, and felt a surge of satisfaction as it hit one of them on the back of the head.

The kid staggered forward and both of them automatically broke into a run, shouting abuse as they disappeared.

Wes's smile fell away though, as Hamdi said, "You feel good? What you just did only makes more trouble for us."

"You said your life here was over anyway." But he looked now and saw how much this young man was struggling to hold it together, and the burden he was carrying. "Look, I'm sorry. I just . . . Okay, this guy you saw hanging around your brother. Did you tell the police about him?"

"I did better than that. I was suspicious, so one day I managed to take a picture of him. I showed it to the police immediately afterwards."

"But nothing happened?"

"Oh, something happened. Both my phone and my computer got hacked and wiped clean." He smiled bitterly, seeing the change in Wes's expression, the increased interest. "Yes, but I'm smarter than them. I store all my university work in the cloud, and I stored the picture there too."

"Can I see it?"

Hamdi looked ready to refuse, possibly thinking that Wes still didn't believe him, resentful of having to prove himself. And to some extent he was right to think that, because Wes *was* skeptical. If an American had been hanging around Hassan Berrada in the weeks before the attack, maybe there was something in that, but Wes certainly couldn't afford to waste time on a grieving brother's conspiracy theories.

Still, Hamdi took his phone and studied it for a minute, tapping the screen, swiping through a few pictures before handing it to Wes. Wes held it up, using his hand to shield the screen from the sunlight, then making sure to keep his face neutral despite the shock of what he saw there.

There were two people in profile talking to each other. One was presumably Hassan Berrada, though he didn't look much like the grainy pictures that had appeared on the news bulletins. The other was clean-cut, wearing chinos and a polo shirt and Wes kind of understood now what Hamdi had meant about him "looking" American.

Wes zoomed in, expanding on the face, hoping to be proved wrong, but the close-up only told him what he already knew. The man looked American because he *was* American, and seeing him in that picture changed everything.

Wes handed the phone back, but Hamdi was studying him carefully, and his tone was accusing as he said, "Who are you? You recognize that man. Who are you?"

"I told you. Rachel was my wife. I used to work for the US government, and yes, I recognize that man, but I don't know his name."

"But you know who he works for?"

Not anymore. The man in the photograph was Scottie Peters, and until three years ago he'd worked for Wes. And Wes was making some immediate assumptions on the back of this discovery but wasn't sure he trusted his own judgment—he needed space, to think it through properly, to be certain in his own mind at least.

Scottie had always looked as clean-cut as he appeared in that picture, a look somehow at odds with his misogyny and his casual racism. Wes had imagined him to be loyal at least, but it seemed the loyalty had also been superficial, transferred now to his new team leader. And that was almost certainly Sam Garvey, which meant Scottie's recruitment of the hapless Hassan Berrada had probably been on Sam's orders.

Hamdi's voice became more strained, more high-pitched, as he said, "You hear me? Do you know who he works for?"

Hamdi was becoming so tightly coiled that Wes started to prepare for things to turn nasty, but he kept his own voice calm as he said, "Yeah, I know who he works for, and as hard as it might be to accept, my advice to you is that you pretend you never saw him."

"You're suggesting the US killed my brother, made him appear a terrorist, and you're saying I should do *nothing*?"

"Yes, for the sake of your family if not for yourself."

"No, I won't do it. And I don't trust you! You're one of them. Why should I trust you? You don't care about us!"

Wes grabbed his shirt at the chest and pushed him against the wall of the building, so hard that Hamdi almost cried out.

"You're right, I don't care about you, but you're not the only person who lost someone here. I lost my wife, and my son is still missing." As he said it, an icy fear coursed through his mind, that Sam Garvey might have Ethan too, but he pushed the thought away. "Now, I have no idea what's going on here. The only thing I can tell you with any certainty is that the man in that picture will be dead very soon. So get smart—help your family rebuild and get on with your life. You hear me? Forget you ever saw him!"

He let go of Hamdi's shirt and stood back, seeing the fear in the younger man's eyes.

"Who are you?" The tone was different this time, and Wes knew he'd said too much, his own anger bubbling to the surface. Wes simply shook his head, because he wasn't sure he had an answer anyway. Who was he? Who had he been, and who was he now?

"We should go back." He started walking, and after a few paces, Hamdi caught up with him. Wes's ankle felt fine now, but the effort of throwing Hamdi against the wall had given him a twinging reminder of the bruised ribs. "I want you to know, most Americans would be outraged by what's been done to your family."

"And yours."

"Maybe."

They walked the rest of the way back without talking.

# Twenty

When they got back into the apartment, Wes could hear someone speaking in halting English. As he walked into the living room he saw it was the woman with the baby, Hamdi's sister. She was talking to Mia, who looked blissfully content sitting there holding an ornate tea glass, apparently oblivious to the context of this visit.

As well as the teapot, there were plates of small pastries sitting on low tables. Mrs. Berrada was looking with a slightly glassy smile at the baby, who was now awake and burbling happily. The two smaller children were sitting on the floor, engaged in some game while Mr. Berrada and the elderly lady looked on with fixed smiles.

Mia said, "Hello, Wes."

"Hello."

"We're having Moroccan tea. It's really good."

"Great. Er, unfortunately, we have to leave."

"Now?" He nodded and she turned to Hamdi's sister and said, "We have to leave now. I hope we can come again. This tea is very nice."

The delivery was once again like someone learning English in an evening class, and Hamdi's sister appeared bewildered by Mia's apparent detachment from the family's all-too-apparent grief.

They said their goodbyes and Hamdi showed them out of the apartment.

Before leaving him, Wes said, "Thanks. That picture changes everything, and I know it's not much of a consolation, but the people who did this, they'll get theirs."

"Will Hassan's name be cleared?"

"No. No, it won't. And you'd be wise not to talk about it with anyone else, as difficult as I know that will be."

Hamdi offered the slightest nod in response, then said, "You still didn't tell me who you are."

"I'm sorry about what happened to your brother, that's all."

Wes turned and followed Mia down the stairs, and once they were walking along the street, she said, "Where are we going?"

He pointed to the busy intersection up ahead. "There's probably a café or bar up there. I need time to think. And I guess we need to talk."

That was enough for her and she walked in silence, with a slightly beatific smile, almost like the one she'd had when she came back from her church visits. She was one of the oddest people he'd ever met and yet he'd miss having her around, but that was what they needed to talk about—and what he needed to think about—because it wasn't safe for her to be with him now.

The pieces had been clattering together in his mind and the scenario that had emerged was about as bad as it could be. Scottie Peters had apparently recruited a gullible young man of limited intellect and duped him into carrying out a terrorist attack in an unlikely location, where one of the victims happened to be the ex-wife of Scottie's former boss.

So, far from being a random victim, Rachel had most probably been the target, and that also meant it had likely been linked to Wes in some way. There was one other possibility, laden with a mixture of guilt and hope—that maybe Rachel had known she was in danger, and that was why she'd spirited Ethan into hiding.

Wes thought of that picture of Scottie talking to Hassan Berrada and felt a searing sense of betrayal. He'd been good to his team, and had fallen on his sword when he could have fought his corner, as much to protect those working for him as to protect the reputation of the Agency and the USA.

Had Rachel been investigating the events surrounding his fall from grace? If so, that would have set her on a dangerous course, to the point where Sam Garvey might have panicked and decided to shut her down. And was Garvey in Spain, too? If not, Wes couldn't understand what Rachel had been doing here, or what she'd planned to do in Málaga.

Wes had something else to consider, and that all depended on what kind of clearance Scottie had received for this mission, and who'd signed off on it. It if had been Sam, that was serious, serious enough for Rachel to go to great lengths to hide her child, serious enough that it wouldn't be safe for Wes to find Ethan until he'd neutralized the threat that Sam posed.

But if Sam had managed to poison the well to the extent that Wes's removal had become an Agency-wide policy, then it might never be safe. Wes guessed he needed to stop thinking about the situation in such sweeping terms—he had to break it down into smaller problems that could be dealt with one at a time, and no matter what the scenario, Sam Garvey would have to be the first of those small problems that Wes tackled.

They'd reached the intersection now and saw a café on the corner. They took a table inside and Wes ordered a coffee. Mia asked for sparkling water. Wes wondered if it was safe for her to take him as far as Madrid, but instantly he realized he couldn't afford to go to Madrid yet—if this was about him, he needed to go in better prepared than he was at the moment. He needed to pay a visit to Patrice's contact in Lisbon first.

"Mia, I think it might be dangerous for you to be with me."

She smiled like he'd said something ridiculous. "People tried to kill you. When you came out of the forest."

He understood what she was getting at, that she'd been aware of the danger associated with Wes from the moment he'd come stumbling and bloodied out of the woods. But the dynamic had shifted violently.

"I'm not sure of the facts yet, but this is what I think happened . . ."

"A hunch."

It wasn't so much that she was being playful, more that she seemed to view life through a filter, with reality always at a step's remove from her idiosyncratic internal universe.

"Kind of, maybe more than a hunch. I think my wife—my ex-wife—was investigating the crime that got me sent to prison and I think she was murdered because of it. Hassan Berrada, he wasn't really a terrorist, he was just a kid who got set up. I think I got set up too, my wife was looking into it, and they killed her. I think she knew she was in danger and that's why she left her son somewhere."

Spelling it out like that made him feel spineless. While he'd been languishing in relative comfort for three years, trying and failing to improve his skills as a painter, Rachel had been trying to clear his name, even after she'd realized it might be putting her life in danger.

"Will you find him?"

"You mean Ethan?"

Mia nodded, but the waitress brought their drinks over, and Wes waited until she'd left them alone again. Mia looked at him expectantly the whole time. It gave him a vital moment anyway, because he'd assured Hamdi that Scottie Peters would be killed, and right now Wes wanted nothing more than to kill him, and Sam Garvey and anyone else who'd been involved in this, but that wasn't his key priority. His key priority was the same as Rachel's had been, to make sure their son was safe.

"Yes, I still plan to find him, but it could be more dangerous than I thought. So I might have to deal with the other side of things first. And no matter what my plans are, these people, they'll be looking for me."

"But they're not looking for me, and we're using my credit cards, not yours, so how can they find you?"

"That's all true, and as long as I keep moving, it might stay true. But they'll be doing everything they can to find me, and if they don't catch up with me in Lisbon, they'll catch up with me in Madrid or the next place. That's why it's dangerous for you."

As if she'd heard nothing of his warnings, she beamed at the mention of Lisbon. "You're going to Lisbon? I can take you there! I've never been before and it's not too far."

"Mia, I can't allow you to do that. You heard what I said. I think it's time for you to go back to Croatia."

She shook her head, simply, as though wanting him to see that he was mistaken.

"I want to stay. My father said I never have to do anything a man tells me. I am my own woman, and I can do what I like. It's a good motto."

"It is, but I really don't think you understand the danger. You might be killed if you stay with me."

"No, I won't. I have faith. I can drive you to Lisbon, but not until morning. I want to visit the cathedral."

He nodded. She was happy. Maybe he'd stumbled into her path at a truly dangerous moment in her own life, after the loss of her father, when she might easily have slipped back into self-destructive ways, but Wes had accidentally given her a purpose, an extra motivation for keeping her promise to the late General. Nor could he deny that she provided him with a cover of sorts.

"Okay." He still had reservations about this, but he was grateful too, that he had found a way of not being alone, that he would keep her as a talisman for the time being. "I won't let anything happen to you."

"Where will we go in Lisbon?"

"We need to visit Patrice's friend."

"The black man."

"That's right."

"Is his friend black, too?"

"I don't know."

She laughed a little. He had no idea what she was laughing at, but he smiled back at her and sipped his coffee.

# Twenty-One

It was early evening by the time they got back to the hotel. Mia went to the cathedral and Wes headed up to his room. He took the envelope that he'd been given in Granada and emptied the contents out onto the bed.

There was the Renfe receipt for two hundred euros, the one for which he'd found no corresponding ticket. Wes didn't like how many conclusions he was drawing, but it was hard not to imagine her traveling by train from Seville to some place unknown on that ticket—what else could it have been for?

What he struggled to imagine was Rachel leaving her son with the friend she'd entrusted him to, knowing she might never see him again. She'd been a shrewd operator in her career, tough-minded, cynical, able to detach herself from the emotion of often-grim situations, but with her own son, she would have surely been devastated.

He found it easier to believe it had been a miscalculation on her part—that she'd known she was in danger, enough to want Ethan somewhere safe, but that she'd honestly believed the threat could be averted and it would be only a temporary separation.

Wes picked up a handful of the postcards, from the cities before Madrid—Barcelona, Salamanca, Toledo—as well as the two that followed her stay in the capital. Some just had random notes written on the back, others were more like small journal entries, and yet Wes saw nothing about Ethan. He understood that, though. It was common in their line of work, being open and relaxed about everything except the things that really mattered.

He noticed a scrap of paper on which she'd written *GB's: 1632*. He guessed that was the entry code for Grace's apartment building in Madrid, so Rachel would have been able to come and go while Grace was at work. Grace would have some answers for him, whether she knew it not, whether she wanted to share them or not, but there was nothing else about her here.

There was also nothing among the various pieces of debris from her last days to hint at the reason for the planned visit to Málaga. That was hardly surprising in a way, because she'd been killed before getting there, but he was intrigued enough by her scheduled brief stop in the city to be certain it was important.

Struck by a thought, he stuffed the postcards and receipts back into the envelope and made his way down to the hotel's small business center. He brought up Google News on the computer and searched for everything he could find on Málaga.

Spotting nothing relevant, he searched again, this time on "CIA" and "Spain," then the more colorful combination of "spy" and "Spain," and then as he scrolled through the results, he spotted a headline and couldn't understand why it hadn't appeared on his first search.

*Russian Spy's Málaga Death Most Likely Natural Causes*

He opened the story. There was a picture Wes never would have recognized, because it looked nothing like the way the man had looked in person. But the name was there too, that of ex-GRU Colonel Konstantin Grishko, who'd died a week ago of a suspected heart attack. He'd been living in Málaga for two years since leaving the GRU—Grishko had only been in his late fifties, so Wes guessed this was yet another person who'd had an early retirement pressed upon him.

Some people had always been skittish about how closely Wes's gray team had worked with Grishko in the Middle East. And relations between Russia and the West had become steadily more toxic in the three years since, to the extent that Sam could have used Wes's dealing with Grishko to tarnish Wes's reputation even further.

More importantly, Grishko had known about someone working for Omar Shadid against the joint interests of both Russia and the US, facilitating the movement of arms and fighters across the Iraqi and Turkish borders into Syria. He'd even hinted more than once that his own intelligence pointed directly to Wes's Baghdad office. He'd probably only held back from naming names to spare Wes's blushes.

So was Grishko also the reason they'd decided to eliminate Rachel? Sam Garvey's guard would have gone up the minute she'd started looking into Wes's case, but if she'd then lined up a meet with Grishko, that would have raised the risk to a whole new level, maybe to the point of doing anything to ensure that meeting never took place.

Sam Garvey had been the rogue element in their operations and now he was running his own gray team, here in Spain or somewhere else in Europe. He'd killed Rachel, he'd killed Grishko, and he would keep trying to kill Wes, because it was the only option—the truth was dangerous for Sam Garvey, so he had no choice but to kill anyone who threatened to expose it.

Wes searched the news stories on the attack in Granada, seeing them in a different light now. There were pictures of some of the victims, and of the scene. He'd seen the pictures of these people before, but he hadn't cared about them then. He probably wasn't alone in that—even among the people who'd been moved at the time, how many would remember these names and faces a few weeks on?

He looked at the broad grin of Garrett Fitzpatrick, a college student from Syracuse, his face full of life and possibility. Wes wanted to see something of his younger self in that face, but he struggled even to remember the person he'd been before all of this.

There, too, was Stephanie Breut, and next to her a picture of her four-year-old son, Oscar, with dark eyes and a mop of dark hair, a dimpled smile. His little body had ended up near Rachel, Wes knew that much—a brief confusion ensuing about whether he might be Ethan.

Wes could find no picture of Rachel, though she was mentioned, of course. She was described as a systems analyst with the State Department, on sabbatical and touring Spain at the time of her death.

It was a shame there was no photograph, because he couldn't quite picture her anymore. He had been able to—he was sure of that—until very recently, and he could recall elements of her face and body but still couldn't picture her, whole, real, as she had once been to him.

What he *could* remember was her voice, the way she'd spoken, the way she'd explained things, always calm and measured. *I know you feel like killing Sam Garvey*, that's what she would have said to him right now, *but you have to focus, J, you have to focus on keeping Ethan safe.* She would have offered a wry smile then, apparently accepting Wes for who he was, and added, *Ethan comes first, but after that, it's your game.*

Of course, Wes wished he could have spoken to her too, to say sorry, to say she never should have tried to clear his name, if that's what she'd been doing. And he'd have reassured her. He was determined to find Ethan. He was Wes's son and Wes would find out where he was and raise him to be the boy she would have wanted. But he'd still deal with Sam first, because as Rachel had learned to her cost, none of them would be safe until Wes did that.

# Twenty-Two

The next day was forecast to be hot, and there was already a threatening warmth in the air when they got into the car to leave early in the morning. Mia handed him something as he fastened his seatbelt. It was Patrice's bible.

"You left it on the back seat. I chose something for you."

"Thanks. I'll . . . take a look."

She smiled, and for a moment he thought she might be waiting for him to open the bible right now—but, satisfied, she turned her attention to the street in front of them, started the car, and pulled away.

She drove with her usual slightly unnerving confidence through the tight streets of the old town, and then, once they were heading out through the suburbs, Wes opened the bible on the page where she'd placed the bookmark.

It was Ecclesiastes, Chapter 3, which Wes immediately recognized, having probably heard it at several funerals over the years— *To every thing there is a season, and a time to every purpose under the heaven: A time to be born, and a time to die . . .*

It was a beautiful passage, but he couldn't help but think it had probably been used at the funerals of some of the victims from Granada, providing false comfort to their friends and families. Maybe it had even been read at Rachel's service.

Then he noticed that Patrice had underlined a small passage in the previous chapter, and his eye was automatically drawn to it.

*Then I looked on all the works that my hands had wrought, and on the labour that I had laboured to do: and, behold, all was vanity and vexation of spirit, and there was no profit under the sun.*

That was a truth Wes could relate to, and understand.

He thought of Patrice's group therapy sessions, and saw how Dr. Leclerc would never be likely to offer any greater guidance than Patrice had found for himself within this book. Every underlined section of text seemed like a staging post on Patrice's path to peace and redemption, and a tantalizing glimpse into the life he'd lived.

Mia's selection was no less interesting. He wondered if she feared for his soul. For that matter, he wondered if Patrice had feared for his spiritual wellbeing, too. They had no need to worry on that account, but it was touching that they did so all the same.

He thought she might question him on the passage she'd selected, but she never mentioned it again. Her mind had apparently moved on and she was fixed now on the road as they drove toward the Portuguese border through a sun-scorched landscape, with fields of grow tunnels looking deceptively like shimmering bodies of water in the distance.

They stopped in a rest area near Faro, then continued toward Lisbon through scrubby and cluttered country threaded with power lines. It was only now that they were getting close to Patrice's contact that Wes started to think about what he would need—it wasn't much, mainly ammunition for the guns he already had, a lock-picking kit if the guy carried that kind of equipment, good-quality handcuffs.

As the thought occurred to him, he said, "You realize, I might have to kill some people."

"In Lisbon?" She sounded unfazed, as if he'd merely said that he might need to go shopping or do some other mundane activity.

"No, not in Lisbon. It's probably the last place they'd look for me. And I might not have to kill anyone, but it's possible, in Madrid or . . . Well, I just think it's best that you know."

"Soldiers have to kill people sometimes, just like the people you killed in the forest."

"That's true." He thought she might say something else, but she seemed remarkably relaxed when it came to the subject of what soldiers might need to do. "Why did your family stop talking to you, your aunts and uncles and cousins?"

"They didn't stop talking. I am the daughter of General Nikola Pavić."

"But you said you weren't close, not since something happened, but you didn't say what?"

Her eyes remained fixed on the road, and for a little while he thought he might have hit a raw nerve and she wouldn't answer, but it seemed she'd simply been thinking through her response.

"My father was a hero. Many people in Croatia consider him this way. Without people like my father, our country might not exist. But the war was not easy, and people outside, they wanted to put him on trial. I persuaded him it was also heroic to go to court, also important for the future of our country. He said he would go to the court, but only if I made a promise to him, that I would eat, and . . ." Almost subconsciously, she removed her hands from the wheel one at a time and pulled her sleeves down over her wrists.

"So that's why your family weren't happy with you?"

"We weren't very close anyway, because of the things they said."

"What kind of things?"

"Cruel things, but we mustn't blame them—they're not very intelligent people. I'm different. My father said I mustn't care about being different, and that I should have sympathy for all the poor people who aren't different at all, who are all just the same as each other."

Wes smiled, wishing he had taken the time to befriend the late General Pavić.

"Your father was a very wise man."

"Yes." Then a moment later, she said, "Have you killed women and children?"

Two of the people in the helicopter that Wes brought down were women, but he guessed Mia was talking about a different kind of crime. More importantly, he guessed she was once again talking about her own father and what might have appeared on his charge sheet.

"The first time I ever killed someone there was a little girl."

"Tell me."

Her curiosity so rarely manifested itself in a way that he recognized that he was thrown now. She wasn't being polite, he knew that much. He was also conscious that he was about to tell Mia something from his past that he'd never even shared with Rachel, in part because she would never have asked, in part because he'd never wanted her to know too much about that side of his life.

"It was in Georgia, in the Caucasus, my first overseas posting. The target was a politician, but a crooked one, in bed with the Russian mafia, secretly helping Moscow undermine his own government. My government decided the only way to guarantee democracy in Georgia was to get rid of him—not quite as simple as you'd imagine. He'd spend every weekend in the country, then head back to the city on Monday morning, and the only weak spot in his security was on that journey between those two houses, so that's where we hit him. We planted a bomb on a rural road—the car was armored but we were confident the bomb would be big enough. I was still pretty junior, so I was the trigger guy, positioned on a hillside up above."

"On your own? On a hill?"

"Sure." She laughed a little, though he wasn't sure what had amused her. "Actually it was beautiful, quite desolate, but beautiful. Anyway, there were other people watching the house, and I got word that it wasn't just him and his driver in the car that morning. For some reason his twelve-year-old daughter was with him. No one was sure what to do, whether to go ahead with it. They were still debating it, but by this time I could actually see the car approaching. Someone told me to stand down, to call off the attack, but I knew we wouldn't get another chance like this. So I ignored them. The car was blown maybe thirty feet into the air, landed on its roof in a field. I could see through my binoculars that the politician was dead, and I guessed the driver was. But the girl, she screamed for ten minutes. I remember being amazed that she could keep screaming like that. I left once she went quiet. They were all dead before anyone else reached the wreckage, I know that much. That was the only time I killed a child."

"Did you get into trouble?"

"I got promoted." Wes laughed, amused by the memory of something that seemed to sum up all that followed, even to the point of becoming an unwitting scapegoat and getting sent to prison. "The mission was considered a success. It wasn't pretty, and I wish the girl hadn't been in the car, but I knew it had to be done, and I guess I was proved right."

"That's why they promoted you. Sometimes a leader has to make difficult decisions."

"That's true."

"And they don't always know what their soldiers are doing."

"That's also true." The parallels were uncanny. Yes, she was talking about her father, but in retrospect it seemed Wes really hadn't known what the members of his own team were doing, and certainly not that they'd been conspiring to get rid of him.

Wes had known about Omar Shadid, but had never considered him important in the maelstrom of everything that was going on in the region—a former Saddam loyalist turned criminal warlord with global ambitions. He'd even approached Wes once, but Wes hadn't been interested. So Shadid had apparently gone to the next person down the chain—the all-too-corruptible Sam Garvey—and in failing to see that danger, Wes had sealed his own fate, and maybe Rachel's too.

"When my father decided to go to The Hague, he told me a general must always take responsibility for the actions of his men."

"I guess so."

"What was her name?"

"Who?"

"The little girl you killed?"

He thought about it for a second. "I don't know."

Had he ever known? It was over ten years ago, and he'd been twenty-six or twenty-seven, swept up in the whole business of being in the field in a complex region. It seemed hard to believe that he'd never seen the girl's name in a news report, as he'd seen Oscar Breut's and Garrett Fitzpatrick's, but if he'd ever known it, he'd forgotten it now.

# Twenty-Three

It wasn't until they were on the approach into Lisbon that Wes thought to ask about where they'd be staying. Mia had, naturally, booked a hotel before leaving Seville, taking rooms in a grand palace on the main avenue in the middle of the city.

As he was checking in, Wes took the envelope Patrice had given him and showed it to the concierge.

"Can you tell me if this address is far from here?"

The concierge studied it and shook his head. "No, it's near the bridge. I'll be able to show you on the map and you can take a taxi."

"We can drive," said Mia.

"Yes, but then you must find somewhere to park. Better to take a taxi, and maybe then you walk a little. And the LX Factory is close by." Neither of them responded to that and he looked at the address again and said, "But I think this is a store, so it might be closed? You know, on Saturday, many stores close at lunchtime."

Wes had lost track of days this week just as surely as he'd lost track of weeks and months during his spell in prison. If the store was closed today it would also be closed tomorrow.

"Okay, thanks. Maybe we can go across to check it out anyway."

"It's worth a try. And if it's closed you can visit the LX Factory so it's not a wasted journey."

They went off to their rooms, and by the time Wes got back downstairs he noticed Mia sitting on one of the many sofas in the middle of the grand atrium that made up the lobby. She was studying her phone but looked up as he got there.

"LX Factory is a real factory! But artists and other people took it over and opened stores and galleries and restaurants. We should go, if your friend's store is closed."

"Sure. You ready?"

She nodded and stood. "In the morning, I go to church. You can come if you like."

"No, I'll leave that to you."

They headed out and picked up a taxi. It only took ten minutes to cross town, but in the heat and with the hilly terrain of the city it would have been a trying walk.

The neighborhood the taxi took them to was either bohemian or down at heel, or maybe both. The cobbled streets were full of ramshackle buildings with graffiti on the doors and the lower walls, plants growing out of the gutters, ornate iron balconies that looked in danger of breaking free. Most of the buildings looked shut-up, but lines of washing hanging here and there between windows spoke of the families within.

The store itself was closed. It appeared to sell T-shirts and baseball caps, but there was no sign of life, and no bell to ring. Twenty yards away a young black guy was sitting on a plastic crate outside a doorway, maybe waiting for someone, maybe just waiting.

Wes walked up to him, showed him the envelope and said, "You know these people?"

He let his eyes drift languidly over the address, looked up at Wes, and shook his head. He was lying, but that was hardly surprising now that Wes thought of it. Everyone in the area probably knew that the T-shirt store was a front for something else, so they were hardly likely to share information about the proprietor with two strange white people who turned up out of nowhere speaking English.

Wes walked away before saying, "We'll have to wait until Monday."

"It's that way." She pointed, and he realized she was talking about the LX Factory.

They set off walking, merging over the last hundred yards or so with other tourists. Wes had seen districts like this in a few different cities around the world, the air of an artists' collective about the place. It was strange to note that Mia, who usually seemed so alien, looked right at home among the people working and socializing here, whereas Wes didn't even blend in that well with the tourists walking wide-eyed around the former factory buildings.

Near the end of their circuit, Mia stopped and stared at a Mexican restaurant, painted with skulls and other Day of the Dead imagery.

She looked for so long that in the end Wes said, "You wanna go in and eat?"

That broke the spell. She shook her head and started walking again, and she kept walking right through the gate and along the street until she noticed a taxi for hire. He didn't know what had disturbed her, but she didn't say anything about it on the ride back, and didn't mention the LX Factory again.

Apart from going to church early the following morning, Mia didn't show much desire to leave the hotel again either, and he wondered if that, too, was a response to the macabre paintings outside the Mexican restaurant. Instead, they spent both afternoons sitting on the modernist white terraces of the sky bar looking out over the city and down to the port. They ate in the rooftop restaurant and then returned to the sky bar, which became livelier still after nightfall.

This was a hipster crowd, though more upmarket than the one they'd encountered at the factory. And once again, he was struck by the fact that Mia looked as if she belonged, like she might be an artist or a musician or a fashion designer. Wes knew that he was the one who didn't fit in so easily—he guessed people would be more likely to assume he was Mia's bodyguard than her boyfriend.

It was a pleasant way to spend a couple of days, and Wes knew it would be confusing Sam Garvey and everyone else. By now they might have worked out that he'd been in Granada and Seville, and they'd be expecting him to turn up in Madrid and getting more nervous with each day that he failed to show. If that had been the only element to consider he'd have been quietly satisfied, but it wasn't.

On Sunday afternoon as they sat looking out over the city and a dazzling blue sky, a family group came out onto one of the terraces below them, including a woman carrying a small boy. Wes didn't have much experience with children and could only guess that the little boy was around the same age as Ethan.

He became instantly agitated, wanting to go back to the T-shirt store right then, even though he knew it was pointless. And he had to tell himself that Ethan was fine. Rachel had put a lot of thought into hiding him away somewhere, and it would have been with people she could trust. Wherever he was, Ethan wasn't waiting to be rescued, to be saved by his unknown father, and yet still Wes could not quieten his unease, or dispel the notion that he was wasting crucial time as he sat there.

# Twenty-Four

It was mid-morning on Monday when they took a taxi back to the T-shirt store. The young black guy was still sitting on his plastic crate a few doors along, looking like he hadn't moved. Three teens were standing outside the store, smoking, laughing, and joking with each other but falling silent as Wes and Mia got out of the car.

They were partly blocking the door, and one of them looked insolently at Wes but seemed to have second thoughts and shuffled aside as Wes approached. The store didn't look open, but when he pushed the door it yielded and set a bell ringing.

A woman came out of a back room and smiled, speaking to them in Portuguese.

"Hi." He held the envelope up. "We're looking for Michel."

She nodded but the smile fell away. She called over her shoulder into the back room, a name Wes didn't quite catch, and then strolled over and sat behind the counter.

A young black guy sauntered out, filling the doorframe. He was wearing a T-shirt with a close-up of a snarling Rottweiler on it, the material taut where it was stretched over his muscles—Wes couldn't remember ever seeing anyone with bigger biceps than this guy.

Wes said, "You speak English?"

"Sure." He didn't look friendly and didn't seem inclined to leave the doorway into the back room.

"Are you Michel?"

"Who are you?"

"I have a letter, for Michel, from a friend."

Wes held it up for him to see. The guy said something in Portuguese to the woman and she came out from behind the counter, took the letter from Wes, and then handed it over. Wes wasn't sure if it was a power play or if he didn't want to leave that doorway—maybe he was just a minder for Michel.

He pointed at Wes now and said, "You, wait there." He smiled, mocking. "Buy some T-shirts."

Once he'd left them, Wes turned to Mia, who was looking expectant and confused.

"He wants us to buy T-shirts?"

"No, he was joking." Mia didn't look convinced. "It wasn't a very good joke. He was trying to show that he's big and he's not afraid of me, that I should be afraid of him, all that crazy macho stuff."

"Will they help?"

"I guess it depends what Patrice wrote in the letter."

He heard movement and turned back to the door. The guy was there again, without the letter, and with a completely transformed demeanor.

"Hey man, sorry about being cagey and all. You know, we have to be careful. You're Wes, right?"

"Yeah, and this is my friend Mia."

"Cool. I'm Rocco. Michel says to come on through. Can I get you a drink or anything?"

"We're good, thanks."

Rocco nodded, offered a real if slightly humble smile, and gestured for them to follow. They walked along a corridor stacked with boxes of stock, then through into an office that was equally

124

cluttered. A man was sitting behind a desk, talking on the phone, but smiling and waving them in, gesturing to the chairs facing him.

He ended the call, then beamed and reached over to shake Wes's hand.

"So good to meet you, Wes. Any friend of Patrice is most welcome here. I'm Michel." He turned toward Mia, hand still outstretched.

"This is Mia. She doesn't like to be touched."

"But of course."

Mia added matter-of-factly, "It's not because you're black."

Michel laughed and Wes turned to her and said, "He knows that."

But Michel said, "Not always true, Wes. I can see your friend is kind, but some people, they see only the color of your skin." Wes nodded, accepting the point. "Now, before we talk, what can I do for you?"

Wes took the list from his pocket and handed it across the desk. Michel opened it and looked.

"Just magazines, no hardware?"

Clearly there was no concern on Michel's part about being under surveillance.

"No, just ammunition."

"And the lock-picking, just manual or electronic too?"

"If you have electronic, I'll take it."

"I have the best." He held out the list and Rocco took it from him and left the room. "Now, how is Patrice?"

"He's well. It's a nice modern prison. He paints, he reads his bible, keeps fit. I think he's happy."

"He has a big heart. A good man." Michel shrugged, as if acknowledging that not everyone would agree with that description. "We'll have a big party on the day of his release."

"How do you know him, Michel?"

"I was in God's Own Army too. Very junior, so for me came rehabilitation, not prison."

Michel was overweight and looked older than Patrice, at least in his forties, but Wes wondered now if he was actually younger. But then, it had been clear from the few stories Patrice had shared that his position within God's Own Army hadn't been earned through seniority.

"And why did you come here? Why not France?"

Michel raised his arms and smiled. "Why would you not come here? It's beautiful, no?" But then he shrugged a little. "We did many bad things, and in France, there are survivors. So . . ."

Wes nodded, understanding. It was better for people like Michel to live far away from the people who might recognize him in the street, point, accuse him of barbarity and the kind of crimes most people did not want to think about.

A bell sounded faintly in the distance, and then light running footsteps coming closer before a small boy burst into the office, knocking on the door only as he was already through it.

Michel laughed and spoke rapidly to the boy, possibly in Portuguese though Wes couldn't be sure. The boy nodded and spoke back, still trying to catch his breath.

Michel looked at Wes now. "You go with him. He'll take you to see a friend of Patrice. You know, we all miss him. We'll have such a party on the day of his release." He nodded to himself. "Yes, you go with the boy. His name is Cristiano, like the football player! And when you come back, everything will be ready."

The boy was already back at the door, bursting with energy, urging them to follow. Wes and Mia went with him, out of the shop and turning up a nearby street. He kept running ahead, then waiting, calling them on.

And then as they turned another corner, Wes caught the unmistakable scent of orange blossom and immediately thought of Rachel. The memory of her made him wish he'd never seen that postcard.

During his time in prison he'd long accepted that he would never see her again, never speak with her again. It had taken the news of her death to show that up as the lie he'd been telling himself. The sense of loss had been growing steadily since, to the point where now he felt her absence painfully. He could smell orange blossom, just as she had in Seville, and there was a terrible emptiness in not being able to share that with her.

# Twenty-Five

The boy led them into a narrower street and then through a door into a garden courtyard at the back of a house. Four trees provided dappled shade for the entire courtyard. There were more children, and two women sitting at a large table preparing food. One was older and wearing traditional African dress, the other—presumably the mother of the children—was dressed in Western style.

They smiled and spoke a greeting, but then a rotund man stepped out of the house, smiling broadly.

"Please, welcome." There were more chairs in a small circle closer to the house and he waved his hands toward them. "You are Wes?"

"Yeah, and this is Mia."

The man bowed his head to Mia, as if he sensed her otherness even without being told, then shook Wes warmly by the hand.

"I am Emmanuel. Please, sit. You are welcome, always."

"Emmanuel? Patrice's friend from his village?"

"Yes."

They sat, but Wes stared at the man, mesmerized. For one thing, he yet again looked older than Patrice, and yet Wes knew they were about the same age. But he'd also assumed that Emmanuel hadn't survived. He thought back to that story Patrice had told, their baptism of fire. Wes had asked what had become of Emmanuel and

Patrice had told him he hadn't ended up in prison. Wes laughed at his own misunderstanding, at the possibility Patrice had deceived him intentionally.

"Please excuse. My English is not so good, but Patrice, he is . . . ?"

"He's very well. He's happy."

Emmanuel nodded, still smiling, but with tears in his eyes, the only indication of the enormity of the history between him and Patrice.

A pretty girl of about ten came out of the dark of the house carrying a tray with three glasses of lemonade on it. She approached Mia first.

"Thank you."

"You're welcome," said the girl, then moved on to Wes and finally Emmanuel.

They all sipped at their drinks, cold and sharp and refreshing, and then Wes said, "Are these children all yours, Emmanuel?"

"No, no. The girl and boy there, they are from Michel. The other three, all mine—Cristiano you already met." He gestured to the table. "My wife. My wife's mother. They prepare food. You will eat with us."

Even as Wes made ready to reply, Mia said, "Thank you. Will it be African food?"

"Oh, some African, some Portuguese."

"Thank you."

Wes looked at Emmanuel, as happy in his own way as Patrice was, though carrying something darker in those smiling eyes.

"How did you come here, Emmanuel? Patrice told me about how you were captured by God's Own Army, but . . . did you come when Michel came?"

"No, I come a long time before. Michel came because I am here already." He looked out at the children playing among the trees of the courtyard, then across at his wife and mother-in-law, working quietly. "Patrice was always stronger. In the body, a little, but in the head, very strong. He always protected me. Many times. He became more powerful and he *believed* because we all believed, but he always kept me close, and when bad things must be done . . . he always protected me. When we were seventeen, already, Patrice became the big leader. And he sent me away. Yes, he sent me away. He believed, but I think already, he began to understand, the things we believed, the things we did, they were not truly God's way. He wanted me to go away, to live. And I came here. God has blessed me. But Patrice—he was God's messenger."

"We are all God's messengers."

Wes turned to look at Mia, who'd been listening rapt and had spoken with a simple certainty he envied.

Emmanuel nodded, slightly bewitched by Mia, and said, "Yes, it's true. We need to be open to the message."

Wes looked between the two of them, conscious that he was the only one not hearing any message at all.

He had to admit to himself, too, that he'd always felt some kind of moral superiority over Patrice and some of the others, General Pavić among them. They had done terrible, barbaric things, whereas even the worst of Wes's actions had been sanctioned at the highest level by a democratic government.

Not only was he less sure now of the difference between their crimes, but there was also this other side to it, the love these people here in Lisbon felt for a man who the world viewed, with good reason, as a monster. Who would speak for Wes in such a way? One person, maybe, and she had died for it.

They sat for nearly two hours over lunch, and while Wes struggled occasionally to find things to say, Mia engaged like a diplomat or a member of some royal family, asking about the different food-stuffs, where they came from, how they were cooked. Wes noticed the children, and to some extent the women, hanging on her every word, staring at her with such intensity that he wondered if they saw the same thing Patrice had, that had led him to think of her as a demon girl.

When they were leaving, Emmanuel insisted that Cristiano would take them, even though they assured him they could remember the way back. And the little boy skipped ahead of them the whole way, singing and calling back to them in Portuguese, and only left them once he'd pushed open the door to the store and set the bell ringing.

Rocco came out to meet them and led them back to the office. Michel wasn't there, but sitting on the desk were two heavy-duty plastic bags with the name of the store on them. A moment later, Michel came bustling in.

"So! You saw Emmanuel? A beautiful family, no?"

"Patrice told me about him, but I didn't realize he was still alive."

"Patrice is a modest man. Emmanuel is alive because of Patrice. Me too, I think." He pointed at the bags. "You see inside, wrapped in T-shirts, but it's everything you asked for. You can check if you like."

"No, I'm sure it's all good. How much do I owe?"

Michel made a look of being stung. "Nothing! Patrice sent you here as a friend. You owe nothing."

Wes shook his hand. "I have no contact details at the moment. When I do, I'll let you have them. If I can ever do a favor for you, it's yours."

"I hope to see you again, that's all. You too, mademoiselle."

They took their leave, getting a taxi back across town. Mia made odd orphaned comments about the episode, suggestive of some internal dialogue to which Wes was granted only random access: "I think one of the trees in the garden was a fig tree," "It was less spicy than I imagined," "It must be a very difficult language to learn."

It was only as they were sitting back in the sky bar later that afternoon, watching the ultra-stylish staff floating around serving an equally stylish clientele, that Mia finally turned her attention to what they'd actually been doing at Michel's store. But even then, she came at it from an oblique angle.

"What will we do with the T-shirts?"

"Oh, there are only four. I might wear them."

She looked astonished. "Like the one with the angry dog!"

"No, they're all plain black."

"Oh." She seemed to think about it. "And tomorrow we go to Madrid."

"Yeah. But . . . I won't keep saying it, but any time you want to . . . to leave, you should. I can travel alone."

"It will take six hours. I checked. We can leave early and be there in the afternoon."

Wes liked those timings. If they made good progress they could be at Grace's apartment in time for her to come home from the embassy. He knew one thing—word would get around quickly once he was in Madrid, so he'd have to act fast, find out what he could, and get out.

"So, tomorrow evening I need to visit someone called Grace Burns. My ex-wife and my son, they stayed with her before going to Seville. She was a friend of my wife. I'm hoping she'll be able to tell me something about what she did with Ethan, maybe even tell me something about what's happening to me."

"Will you kill her?"

"No. Of course not. I don't want to kill anyone. But Grace is CIA, so . . ."

So what? She might try to kill him, she might overreact and force Wes into doing the same? Why did it matter what she did? He had no intention of killing her, not if he could help it.

"Sometimes soldiers have to kill people."

It was no less true than on the other occasions she'd said it. Sometimes soldiers had to kill people. Sometimes they wanted to kill people and didn't. And sometimes the decision was taken for them.

# Twenty-Six

He looked in Grace's fridge. It was well stocked and there was a bottle of white wine in the door, unopened.

For some reason, he thought of today's passage from the bible. Without comment, before leaving Lisbon, Mia had handed him the bible, and sure enough the bookmark had been moved, and she had selected a chapter from Proverbs for him.

*Wisdom hath builded her house, she hath hewn out her seven pillars . . .*

But a few lines into the passage, a single underlining in pencil showed that Patrice had been there before either of them, in dialogue with himself, but his selections no less meaningful for that.

*Forsake the foolish, and live; and go in the way of understanding.*

Patrice had achieved that. For his own part, Wes felt maybe he was still a work in progress.

He took another look in the bedroom and the bathroom, even though he'd been through them once. He looked in the guest bedroom again too, though he didn't want to linger in there, then strolled back into the living room, where Mia was sitting facing the doorway.

She glanced from side to side, moving only her eyes, the look of someone who feared they might be reprimanded in some way for breaking the rules.

"Is this really okay? Won't she be angry?"

"Well, I guess she won't be happy. No one likes strangers breaking into their apartment."

"But you said you know her."

"I know her a little. She was Rachel's friend, not mine. You're a stranger." He was teasing her, but she didn't react and then another truth presented itself to him. "Actually, she'd probably be more relaxed about you being here than she would me." Mia nodded. "I'm just being light-hearted. Really, it'll all be fine."

"Really?"

"Really." She glanced down at the gun he was holding casually by his side. "Don't worry. The gun is just for protection. She'll probably have a gun herself. But don't think about that—it'll be fine."

He sat down and placed the gun on the coffee table next to the cuffs. Mia looked at them, frowning, but whichever puzzle was occupying her mind, she didn't share it.

They sat in silence for about fifteen minutes, and then Wes heard the faint sound of someone talking and ascending the steps to this floor. He took the gun and jumped up, holding his finger to his lips for Mia's benefit.

He moved quickly through the apartment and stood to the side of the front door. He could hear clearly enough now to be pretty certain it was Grace; another moment and he could tell that she was talking on the phone. He heard her say, "I've got a bottle in the fridge," the suggestion that the person on the other end was coming over at some point in the evening.

She ended the call before opening the door, used her foot to kick it shut behind her, and headed through to the living room. Wes fell in behind her and noticed her body language shift violently as she saw Mia sitting facing her.

Mia said, "Hello."

Grace didn't respond directly, reaching into her purse instead, fumbling, presumably going for her gun, her phone clattering to the floor in the process. Grace's role at the embassy probably didn't require her to be armed on a daily basis. There was a good chance she was carrying now only in response to the perceived threat from Wes. If that was the case it was inexcusable that she'd been so complacent when she'd first come into the apartment, and that her gun was in her purse rather than on her person.

"Keep your hand in the purse, Grace." She twitched in reaction to his voice behind her, but stopped herself from turning. He nudged the silencer into her back and reached with his other hand to take the purse from her. "Slowly, take your hand out. If there's anything in it, anything at all, I'll drop you right here."

"Okay, Wes, don't do anything stupid."

He felt like shooting her for that comment alone, but he watched as she eased her hand free and splayed the fingers to show that it was empty. He held on to the purse, nudged her in the back.

"Sit in the armchair."

As she moved forward he looked into the purse. The gun was in a holster buried among the clutter of her daily life. He guessed she'd been told to carry it, told of the risk, but maybe the last couple of days had been enough for her to drop her guard, convince herself that he wouldn't show up here after all.

She moved over and sat as Wes put the purse down in the corner.

"What are the cuffs for?"

"I wasn't sure if I'd need them or not. Maybe I don't."

He sat down on the opposite end of the couch from Mia, enough room for an extra person between them. Grace was facing them, no longer looking like the person he remembered. She had always had an austere look about her, and an attitude that he could best describe as pinched, whereas Rachel had been more passionate, more joyous, despite the rigors of the job she'd done. That's why he'd found it so hard to imagine them as friends.

But Madrid appeared to agree with Grace Burns. Her skin was a little tanned, her hair a shade lighter and more relaxed in style, her figure a little fuller. He could picture her with Rachel now, though that only caused a tight ball of anger to lodge in his stomach.

"Are you going to kill me, Wes?"

"Why would I do that?"

For a moment, she looked as if she feared she might have made a mistake, but then she developed a look of resolve and said, "It's what you do, isn't it—why you went to prison? The way I heard it, you were pretty much out of control by the end."

So this was the narrative Sam Garvey had written for him.

"No, I wasn't out of control. In retrospect, it looks like I lost control of my team, in more ways than one, but I was always focused on the job."

"Focused—that's what you call it?"

He appreciated her determination to come out fighting, but he still didn't like her tone.

"What have you heard, Grace?"

"More than I'd like. How about four years ago? Three Turkish border guards, killed by an ISIL car bomb, but it wasn't ISIL, it was you. The same week, the local police chief was shot dead and apparently that was you too. In fact, I'm told in that particular instance it was actually you who pulled the trigger. So, do you call that being in control, doing ISIL's work for them, killing NATO allies?"

"Nice try, Dr. Leclerc." Understandably, she looked confused and even a little rattled by his private joke. Maybe Wes was rattled, too, because Sam had been smart to focus on real events, simply casting them in a sinister light. "I'm sure nothing I say will change the view that's been spread through the Agency, but I feel honor bound to correct you in this particular case. See, for months we'd had a problem with ISIL fighters crossing and recrossing the Turkish border with impunity, costing a lot of lives in the process, particularly among our Kurdish colleagues. Our sources pointed to the police chief, as you refer to him, and to a small unit of border guards working with him. We eliminated all four of them and the problem ceased almost overnight. More importantly, under my watch, nobody outside of George Frater and the members of my gray team knew anything about our involvement. Do you call that out of control?"

"It's not the only story."

"Oh, I'm sure. Who replaced George Frater?"

"Aaron Schalk. I don't know if he took responsibility for George's gray teams, but he replaced him." She glanced across the room to the spot where her cellphone had settled on the floor. "If you wanna hand yourself in, he's probably the man."

"Hand myself in? For what? Why am I an Agency target?"

"Do you need to ask? Wes, you killed the detail that was sent to collect you from prison."

"You really think they were sent to collect me?" She didn't answer. But that also suggested the hit against Wes had been entirely Sam's doing rather than something sanctioned at a higher level—though as Grace had pointed out, that was academic now that he'd killed three CIA officers. "Where's Sam Garvey?"

"I don't know. I know the name, obviously, but I don't know him. I don't know anything about his operations."

"Where's Scottie Peters?"

"No, I don't know that name at all." She was lying. Most people would have missed it, but Wes could tell she was lying about Scottie Peters, which meant he was probably in Madrid. "What is it you want, Wes?"

"How long till your friend arrives?"

138

"Excuse me?" He didn't respond and she looked at her watch. "Maybe twenty minutes."

"Where's my son?" She shook her head. "Did you know they planned to kill Rachel?"

"No! How . . . how could I? Of course I didn't know."

"So why didn't she trust you? She stayed here, what, two days, three days? She didn't tell you she was trying to clear my name, she didn't tell you she feared for her life, she didn't entrust you with the safety of our son?"

He'd been guessing at some of that, but Grace's lack of an answer told him enough, and then she came back combatively. "What makes you think he's your son anyway?"

"I'm on the birth certificate."

"That doesn't prove anything."

She had a point, but in a moment of clarity, he saw a more obvious truth.

"She wouldn't want to claim me as the boy's father if it weren't true."

She yielded in silence, and for a while it looked like she might not reply at all, but then she shook her head—what appeared to be a genuine response to the situation she'd found herself in.

"I suspected she might be in danger. I knew she was looking into your case, and that it wasn't wise. I didn't know they'd kill her, I still don't know for sure that's what happened, but I'll admit, it seems too much of a coincidence that someone asking awkward questions should . . . well, should die like that."

"She wasn't asking questions that were awkward for the Agency, she was asking questions that were awkward for Sam Garvey, and the silence of the rest of you has allowed him to kill Rachel and a dozen other people—and Rachel's son would have been one of them if it hadn't been for her foresight. I want you to think about that, Grace, the little boy who was here in this apartment just a few weeks back. He would've been blown to pieces like the rest of them. I'm amazed that you think I was out of control but Ethan's murder would have been acceptable to you."

"I didn't say that! I wouldn't have . . . I wouldn't . . ." He could see, somehow, that she was thinking of Ethan now, becoming emotional. "I wouldn't have let anything happen to Ethan."

"Yes, you would. Just like you let it happen to Rachel."

"It wasn't like that!" As if realizing Wes was playing her, she visibly regrouped. "Look, Wes, if Sam Garvey broke the rules—"

"*If?*" She looked nervous about responding. "I had an idea someone in my team was rotten. Sam would've been the last person I suspected at the time, what with being one of my best friends and all, but it was him. He was selling us out. He feared I was closing in on him, so he made sure I got false information about that helicopter, set me up for a fall. Rachel started looking into it, got too close, she gets killed. She'd tracked down a GRU colonel I worked with and guess what, he dies a week later, suspected heart attack. I get released from prison and three people come to kill me. Sam Garvey didn't just break the rules, he broke the rulebook."

"May I use your bathroom?"

Wes and Grace both turned to look at Mia, and Grace said, "Sure, like I have a choice."

Mia smiled and left the room, then Grace turned back to Wes.

"Your new girlfriend? You took a real step down from Rachel, didn't you, Wes."

"Is Sam Garvey still in the Middle East?"

"I told you, I don't know. I wouldn't tell you if I did and you wouldn't expect me to, but I don't know anyway."

"Scottie Peters persuaded a vulnerable young Muslim man to carry a backpack, thinking he was on a mission for the CIA, which he was, in a way. Scottie killed that young man and a dozen other people, including three children and my wife—your friend."

She looked exasperated.

"I don't know what you want from me, Wes. I told you before, I've never heard of anyone named Scottie Peters."

Wes shot her in the leg, just below the knee.

# Twenty-Seven

She cried out, but it was muted, a determination not to look defeated—he admired her for that. He waited for her to recover from the shock, to deal with the pain.

"I meant what I said, Grace, I don't want to kill you. Let's go back to something easy: did Rachel give any indication to you that she had plans for Ethan?"

Grace shook her head, then looked down at her leg and stifled a cry.

"Wes, I need . . . My leg . . ."

He looked down at it himself. He'd hit the top of the calf muscle, but he'd missed the bone, and given that the wound wasn't bleeding too heavily, he guessed he'd missed the artery too.

"Your leg's okay. What about Rachel?"

She shook her head. "I had no idea."

"And the Agency really has no clue where he is?"

"None. Whatever she did, she did it well. It's been the talk of the office since the attack. Apparently they had a tracker on her suitcase and a lock on her cellphone, but she never diverted from her itinerary."

Wes thought of the case sitting in Rachel's Seville hotel room, the phone left on charge. She'd have known to leave the cellphone behind. Whether leaving the suitcase had been entirely an intentional ploy or whether she'd just wanted to travel light, that decision had masked her movements perfectly.

"So she fooled you all. Still got killed."

"I swear I didn't know." She closed her eyes, looking faint with a wave of pain, then opened them again as Mia walked back in.

"You have a very nice bathroom."

"Thanks, I guess. It was like that when I moved in."

Mia pointed. "You have blood on your leg."

"Yeah? That's because your boyfriend just shot me."

Mia looked at Wes, and laughed. To Grace it would have looked deranged, as if Mia were laughing at the violence. Wes already knew her well enough to know that she was laughing at the description of him as her boyfriend.

He turned his attention back to Grace. Ethan's whereabouts had been the talk of the office, which meant he could probably rule out once and for all that Garvey had him. But that didn't help Wes to find him.

As if reading his thoughts, Grace said, "What is it you want, Wes? You want to find Ethan? Isn't it obvious she didn't want you or anyone else to find him? I don't want to hurt your feelings, but it looks like she didn't want you to have anything to do with him. She didn't even tell you he existed."

"I was in prison."

It wasn't much of a response and she didn't bother to answer it directly. "Wes, it's clear she got him somewhere safe, somewhere she wanted him to be. She didn't want you to find him. That's the only explanation. So what's left—you want revenge against Sam Garvey, Scottie Peters, anyone else involved?"

"So you do know who Scottie Peters is."

"What does it matter? Yes, I know who he is, but I don't know him. I know Sam Garvey runs a gray team but I don't know where—"

"Here in Spain?"

"No, I would know if it was in Spain. Peters was here on his own." She looked earnest, concerned, though maybe that was just the pain from her knee. "Wes, if you're telling the truth, there are channels for dealing with what happened. Going after Garvey's team, it just isn't an option."

"Isn't it? I guess I've killed three of them already. That probably only leaves four or five more."

"Are you serious? Listen to yourself. You're trying to tell me you weren't out of control in the Middle East and in the next breath you're talking about killing five more people. Why? In revenge for what they did to you or what they did to Rachel?"

"I don't know. It just feels right, I guess. And Sam seems intent on killing me, so I don't really have much of a choice. I want my son, and I can't have him as long as Sam's still in the picture."

Mia said, "Someone's coming."

He cocked his head, amazed that Mia had heard anything, but Grace said urgently, "Wes, please, whatever your plans, he's not armed. I'm just . . ."

Her words dried up as Wes looked at her, but then he put his finger to his lips, letting her know that she needed to remain silent if she wanted this to end well. A key sounded in the lock, so this was a boyfriend, and Wes found it slightly sickening to see how desperate Grace was to preserve her own shot at future happiness.

"Hey! I brought another bottle just in case. I'll put it in the fridge." They heard him walk through into the kitchen, but he kept talking from there. "I swear to God, if that guy stays any longer, I'm moving in with you. Two weeks, they said!" Wes looked at Grace and smiled, spotting this as the likely lucky break he wanted. Grace looked stony-faced in response. "Babe?" His footsteps approached and then he appeared and saw Mia first, a double take before he smiled. "Hello?"

"Hello."

But his smile had already dropped because he'd come into the doorway now and seen Wes, and Wes made sure he saw the gun too. There was an upright wooden chair against the wall and Wes nodded toward it.

"Pull that chair over, sit next to Grace. You try anything, the first thing I'll do is shoot her in the stomach."

He nodded, compliant and nervous. He was young and clean-cut, probably from the cultural section or some other department whose employees didn't regularly get guns pointed at them. He moved the chair, but halted briefly and rocked back on his heels as he noticed Grace's leg.

As he sat down, he reached out to her. She squeezed his hand but let it go again, and looked earnestly at Wes.

"Noah doesn't have anything to do with this. I—"

Wes looked at him. "You're Noah?"

"Yeah."

"I'm Wes. Hello." Noah nodded in response and Wes turned back to Grace. "I thought you didn't have anything to do with it either?"

"I didn't, but I know that's not how you see it—my job, the fact that me and Rachel were friends, I get it. You're blaming me for what happened to her."

He ignored her.

"What's your surname, Noah?"

"Porter."

"So, Noah Porter, why did they move Scottie Peters in with you?"

Noah looked panicked, turning to Grace, hoping for guidance, though she only shook her head to show she had nothing for him. It had been a guess on Wes's part, but he doubted many people had turned up in Madrid over the last few weeks seeking government accommodation.

"I . . ."

"Grace will need an operation on that leg. She may end up with a limp. But I need you to understand, that will be the least of her problems if you don't start answering my questions."

"I have a two-bedroom apartment, but my roommate moved out in January, so it's just me. They needed something quick."

"Mia, in the kitchen there's a notepad and a pen on the counter. Would you get it for Noah, please?"

"Yes."

She got up and left the room.

"I want you to write your address down for me. Now, I have a list of the embassy employees and their addresses, so this is just to save time. If I cross-reference and you've lied, I'll come back here and kill both of you. Understand?"

Noah nodded. "But he won't be there. He goes to the gym."

"What time?"

"He goes about seven, comes back sometime after eight."

Wes checked his watch. It was approaching seven thirty, so if anything Wes wouldn't have too much time on his hands.

"Does he walk or drive to the gym?"

Mia came back in and handed the pad and pen to Noah as if she thought this a completely normal situation. She sat again.

"Thanks, Mia."

"You're welcome, Wes."

Noah looked between the two of them, then said, "Er, he drives. I don't have a car, so he uses my parking space."

He started to write on the notepad.

"Your parking space?"

"It's a modern apartment building near the cathedral. There's an underground parking garage."

From the corner of his eye, Wes could see Mia stir in response to that. "Do you go to the cathedral?"

He tore off the top sheet of the notepad and handed it to Wes as he said, "I beg your pardon?"

"She asked if you went to the cathedral—I think it's a pretty simple question."

"No, I haven't. I . . . I'm sorry, I don't know what you want from me."

"You're doing fine, Noah. Scottie ever talk about what he's doing here?"

"No."

"Okay, empty your pockets onto the table here, take off your watch, your belt. Grace, take off any jewelry."

They did as he said, Grace with resignation, Noah with a growing appearance of confusion and fear. Once they'd finished, Wes picked up the cuffs and pointed to Grace's left hand. She held it forward and he fastened one of the cuffs around her wrist.

"Okay, Mia, you can wait here. You two, let's visit the bathroom."

"I can't walk."

"Yes, you can. Noah will help you."

They stood and Noah helped her into the bathroom. It wasn't large, but it was perfect for what Wes had in mind, not least because of the sturdy sink resting on a pedestal.

"Okay, Grace, on the floor there, slip your hand behind the sink pedestal."

Noah helped her down, then stood again and turned to Wes.

"You want me to sit on the other side?" He'd probably just begun to realize Wes wasn't going to kill them, and his resulting air of compliance was steeped in gratitude.

Wes patted him down, then pointed with the gun. Noah got down onto the floor and put the other cuff on his own wrist. Wes crouched down to check it was tight enough and secure. He stepped back then and looked at the two of them sitting cramped with their backs against the wall, hands linked behind the pedestal. In that position it would be hard to pull the pedestal away from the wall anyway, and neither of them looked possessed of any great strength.

Wes went into the kitchen and turned off the water supply, then went back into the bathroom and closed the window. He removed their shoes and threw them out into the hallway. He sat on the edge of the tub then.

"I've turned off the water, so flooding the apartment below isn't an option. You could shout and scream, try to attract attention, or you could work at getting the pedestal away from the wall—looks pretty solid though. Failing that, I guess when you don't show up for work in the morning, someone will come investigate."

Still wearing her professional hat and determined to try one last attempt at talking him down, Grace said, "What are you gonna do, Wes?"

"Oh, I think you know the answer to that." He looked at his watch again. "Now, I need about forty minutes. So you have a dilemma. If you escape before then and mess up my plans, but don't mess them up enough, I'll track you both down and I'll kill you. If you wait forty minutes before trying to escape or raise the alarm, you'll never see me again." He pointed at Grace with the gun. "You know I'm taking a risk by leaving you alive, and you know I don't take risks. So be smart. I want the two of you to have a chance at the life I didn't get to live."

In truth, it wasn't much of a risk—it would take them more than forty minutes to get out of there. And Grace cared enough about Noah Porter that she'd make sure of it.

Wes stood and headed out of the bathroom, but stopped when Grace said, "Wes!" He turned. "I didn't know. I'm so sorry about what happened to her. But I didn't know."

He stared back at her for a second but could find nothing to say. He walked to the living room. Mia was staring with fascination at the various items on the coffee table, but she looked up now and smiled at him. Wes smiled, too, as he took Noah's keys off the table.

"We need to go."

"Okay." She stood and followed him out and it wasn't until they were on the street again that she said, "Where will we go now?"

"I need you to go back to the hotel. I'll be away for a few hours, but then we have to leave Madrid. I know you probably wanted to visit the cathedral." She nodded. "It'll have to wait until some other time."

"I'll wait at the hotel for you."

"Yes. It could be late, maybe even after midnight, but I'll be back."

"Then we'll leave. And we haven't really been here at all."

"Yeah, I guess that's the point. But you can come back to Madrid someday."

"Those people." She looked over her shoulder as if expecting to see Grace and Noah following them down the street. "They were very scared of you."

"They thought I might kill them."

149

"No." She laughed. "They were *very* scared of you, like you might do something worse."

"Worse than killing them?"

"Maybe."

He nodded. "Yeah, I can see that."

Maybe there were some benefits to having such a terrible reputation, no matter how unjustified it was. Sam had convinced everyone that Wes had been out of control, and ironically, Grace and Noah had undoubtedly been more compliant than they would have been if they hadn't believed that version of events. Scottie Peters knew the truth, so he wouldn't have the same fear, but Scottie was going to die anyway.

# Twenty-Eight

Noah's apartment block was an anonymous modern building that could have been just about anywhere. So it looked particularly out of place sitting halfway between the heart of the old town and the cathedral.

It was just before eight when Wes got there, and still light, the streets full of daytime tourists as well as people dressed for the evening ahead. No one paid any attention when he headed down the ramp into the underground garage.

There was no security, and despite the modernity of the building, there were no cameras in there either. Most of the parking spaces were occupied, but Wes could see the gap that was assigned to Noah's apartment, so he knew Scottie was still out.

He looked around and spotted a door into a boiler room. He worked the lock, stepped inside, and closed the door so it allowed a view over just a narrow strip of the garage, including the empty space that interested him.

He settled in for the wait then. A car came in after a few minutes but it was an older man and Wes didn't see where he parked. He heard him getting out of the car, whistling tunelessly and taking the elevator.

Ten minutes later, a dark blue Lexus pulled into the garage and eased into the empty space. The engine stopped and the trunk popped open, but at the same time, Wes could hear the elevator whirring into action. That could complicate things—Wes really needed Scottie to be on his own down here. But if it came to it, Wes didn't think it would be too difficult to take him in the apartment.

The driver's door opened and Scottie got out, still in his gym clothes—knee-length shorts, a fresh-looking T-shirt that didn't suggest he'd done much in the way of a cardio workout. He ambled to the back of the car but the elevator doors opened out of Wes's eyeline and Scottie looked across.

"Hey, how's it going?"

Wes guessed it was a woman, and that Scottie still hadn't lost his tendency to hit on every female he encountered. It was a scattergun technique that had brought him a fair amount of success in that department, in among all the understandable rebuffs from women who probably recognized a predator when they saw one.

"Very well, thank you." She spoke with a Spanish accent, her tone formal rather than friendly.

The sound of her heels clacked on the floor but she didn't come into view.

Scottie was staring determinedly in her direction and said, "Just back from the gym."

"Yes, I can see that." She laughed a little, nervously. "Have a nice evening."

"Sure, you too." He continued to watch as she got into her car and started the engine. He looked irritated when he finally gave up and turned back to the trunk of his own car, like he couldn't work out why she'd been so aloof with him.

Wes was already thinking of backup plans—following Scottie to the elevator or waiting until he was settled in the apartment, maybe in the shower. But Scottie appeared to be taking his time, sorting through something in his gym bag, and then the woman's car glided past at a decent speed, the engine noise raising a notch as it fired up the ramp.

Wes didn't wait. Using the cover of the car's departure and Scottie's preoccupation with his gym bag, he pushed out of the boiler room. He walked quickly, maybe ten steps, the gun at his side in case he needed it. Wes was maybe a step or two away when Scottie sensed a presence and started to turn, but not with alarm, not with the air of someone who thought he was being threatened.

Wes moved fast, locking his hand onto the back of Scottie's neck and slamming his head forward into the edge of the raised trunk lid, producing a fleshy crunch. Scottie threw himself back into his assailant, and swung his arm with force, landing a blow on Wes's neck that was so hard it felt like it had cut off the blood supply.

Scottie continued to turn as Wes staggered backward, but Wes knew he couldn't afford to let Scottie get the upper hand now. He threw his weight into Scottie's body. Scottie lashed out blindly, but Wes had the momentum now, driving him forward until he crunched into the car again and his upper body smashed down into the trunk space.

Wes gave him a couple of sharp hard punches to the side of his face as he landed, and before Scottie had registered what was happening, Wes had the gun barrel pushed up under his jaw and a knee on his back.

"Move and I'll shoot you right here."

"Wes?" He sounded surprised, but confused rather than fearful.

Wes reached for his second pair of cuffs, slipping one quickly onto Scottie's right wrist. Realizing what was happening, Scottie started to struggle again, so Wes pushed the gun deeper into his flesh. He felt like driving the barrel right up under Scottie's jaw and through the inside of his skull.

He was surprised by how much anger he felt toward the stricken man beneath him. He knew it wasn't entirely justified. Scottie would have been ordered to kill Rachel, and would since have been spun the line that Wes had gone rogue, as shown by his killing of Pine and his colleagues. But Scottie had a mind of his own, he knew the kind of boss Wes had been, and he should have gone above Sam to question why Rachel was being targeted.

Wes cracked him over the head with the gun, not hard enough to knock him out but hard enough to stun him for a second or two. He used that moment to cuff the other hand so his arms were pinned behind his back. Wes pulled the gym bag free and out onto the garage floor, then heaved Scottie's legs into the car. And now, for the first time, Scottie was staring at him, his mouth and nose bloodied, his eyes unfocused.

Wes kept an eye on him as he bent down to the gym bag, and he understood now why Scottie's T-shirt had been so pristine. There was another one inside the bag, still sweat-soaked—Wes took it out and tore it.

"Wes, this is insane." Whatever Wes had done to his face with that first blow, Scottie's voice sounded groggy, like he'd just come back from a visit to the dentist. "I don't know what—"

Wes tied the torn T-shirt around Scottie's head, and Scottie cried out as it tightened against his injured mouth. Wes looked in the pockets of Scottie's shorts and found the car's key fob but nothing else. He closed the trunk.

Wes knew Scottie wouldn't go to the gym without his cellphone—he checked the bag, and found it there. There was a lock on it, and he knew he wouldn't get that information out of Scottie, so the benefits of finding any clues within the phone were probably outweighed by the risk of Sam Garvey and the rest of the team using it to trace their location.

He put it down and kicked it skittering under the neighboring cars. Then he got in, started the Lexus and reversed out of the space. It was only as he drove up the ramp and out onto the street that he realized he hadn't driven a car in over three years—he'd forgotten how much he enjoyed it.

# Twenty-Nine

He was unhurried as he drove through the city because he wasn't sure where he was going. He wanted to avoid the freeway and he wanted to get out of town, but that was all he knew. Mia would have probably driven with her usual speed and confidence and taken Wes to exactly the right place.

Within forty-five minutes he found himself in an area that seemed promising. There were houses here and there, or small isolated buildings that seemed suggestive of some agricultural industry or other, but they were set amid a sprawling area of patchy forest, the trees low, the ground bare between them.

Now and then, tracks would lead off the narrow road, and Wes turned onto one of them and drove steadily uphill for a mile or more without seeing any indication that it led to a farmhouse or any other habitation.

The sun was setting now and there was already a promise of twilight in among the low trees, which seemed denser here as the ground undulated ever upward away from the road. Wes stopped and switched off the engine.

And then he heard some indistinct click and looked in the rearview to see the trunk opening. He released his seatbelt, grabbed the gun from the passenger seat, and jumped out of the car. Scottie was already out and running, disappearing into the trees, and Wes could see that somehow he'd managed to get the cuffs from his back to his front—any other time, he'd have admired him for that.

Wes set off after him. Scottie was zigzagging in the hope of avoiding a bullet, so Wes made quick progress at first, narrowing the gap between them to the point where he could probably shoot and stand a decent chance of hitting Scottie in the leg. But then the trees became denser still and suddenly Scottie disappeared from sight.

Wes stopped. Now that he was out of the car he realized how hot it was, a wall of heat, and all he could hear was the buzzing of cicadas, like radio interference spread across the landscape. The light was already fading—within another half hour or so it would be dark.

He turned slowly, looking out for any sign of movement. He listened too, though beyond the claustrophobic barrage of the cicadas he knew he'd be unlikely to pick up the sound of Scottie running. There was no sign of him, and Wes was pretty sure that meant he was standing still somewhere, relying on the complexity of the landscape to protect him.

Even so, Wes remained vigilant, conscious that Scottie now had his arms in front, and that, even cuffed, he could do Wes some damage if he surprised him. In another moment of paranoia, he checked that he'd slipped the key fob for the Lexus into his pocket—the last thing he needed was Scottie outflanking him and taking the car.

He edged forward, moving slowly enough that he'd spot any movement. The wall of noise from the cicadas seemed to come in waves, and in one of the lulls Wes heard the sound of a vehicle a long way off, probably on the road he'd left to get here.

And that was when he saw him, no more than a fleeting shadow in the deepening gloom, suggesting he'd kept moving for a while after Wes had stopped, because he was more than a hundred yards away now. Scottie had apparently heard the car, too, because he was running down the low incline, making desperately for the road.

Wes sprinted after him and almost immediately regretted it, his foot buckling slightly under the ankle he'd injured a week before, sending a twinging reminder of that earlier discomfort. He changed his pace, running gingerly now for fear of doing more damage.

He couldn't even understand why Scottie had broken cover. The passing car was too far away, and even if Scottie got to the road before Wes caught him, it would be long gone. As his former boss, Wes felt like debriefing him, asking him why he hadn't simply sat tight until darkness had fallen.

Scottie was gaining momentum as he ran downhill. Wes kept to a steady pace, even as he sensed the gap growing between them, and then he spotted Scottie lose his footing and hurtle forward, almost cartwheeling into the ground. Even with the background humming of cicadas, Wes could hear his body thumping the dry earth and the air being pummeled out of his lungs.

Wes kept his eyes on the spot as he ran on. Scottie scrambled back to his feet, fell again. He climbed back onto his knees and readied himself for one more effort, but Wes was on him now and he knew it. At the last, Scottie fell back hopelessly. Wes had slowed to a walk, still approaching with caution as Scottie shuffled across the ground and positioned himself with his back against a tree.

The torn T-shirt that Wes had used to gag him now hung around his neck like a scruffy neckerchief. He'd lost a sneaker, too, maybe in the fall. He looked like someone who'd crashed out of a marathon.

In the gathering twilight, Wes was right in front of him before he noticed that Scottie's eyes were closed. He didn't seem out of breath, and yet Wes felt his own lungs burning, his heart pounding against his rib cage. Up close, Scottie looked more composed, a meditative quality about him.

Wes looked around, saw a tree facing Scottie's resting place, checked the ground for snakes, then lowered himself against it. They were only about ten feet apart, two former colleagues, resting in the evening after a hard day.

Wes could still hear the car somewhere in the distance, its position and direction so hard to determine that it only reinforced how crazy Scottie had been to make a run for it.

"You never would've made it to the road, Scottie. You shouldn't have broken cover."

Scottie nodded, apparently conceding the mistake, and finally he opened his eyes. Now that Wes was at rest, his vision was adjusting to the gloom and he could see Scottie more clearly—he looked resigned, beaten, and yet there was something still defiant about him.

"You wouldn't have given up." His mouth still sounded full of cotton wool—Wes had messed his face up pretty bad with those first couple of strikes.

"Where's Sam Garvey?" Scottie shook his head, making clear what Wes already knew—nothing would make him talk. "I had to ask, but I respect your loyalty. Shame you didn't show a bit more to me."

"I was loyal, Wes, but you became impossible to follow. And then you went to prison. I work for Sam now."

"I became impossible to follow? Yet you were happy to kill a handful of civilians as cover for the murder of an Agency employee who just happened to be asking questions that Sam Garvey didn't like. I became impossible to follow but you were happy to do that without a moment of doubt."

Scottie sat for a few seconds, shaking his bowed head, apparently in dialogue with himself. When he met Wes's gaze again, he looked resolute.

"I did you a favor. I killed her before she found out what a psycho you are."

This was wrong. Scottie had no excuse for talking like that. This wasn't someone who'd been spun a line by Sam Garvey, this was someone who'd worked for Wes, who knew him. Had Scottie always thought of him as a psycho, or was it the result of revisionism in his own mind, to justify what he'd done in Granada?

"Dress it up however you like, Scottie, but I know the truth. You killed Rachel before she found out Sam and the rest of you sold me down the river."

Scottie laughed like a drunk. "You still don't get it, do you? We stayed loyal to Sam for a reason."

"All of you? The whole team?" Scottie didn't respond, probably not wanting to give Wes anything he could use. "Even Harrod and MacPherson?"

"I'm sure they would've done. They were killed in a car accident outside of Erbil."

"Of course they were. How convenient. Oh, I'm sure Sam was torn up about that."

"He was. Sam looked out for us!"

"So did I."

"Yeah?" He stared hard at Wes, the seconds creeping past, his face full of anger, or maybe just contempt. "Like you looked out for Davey Franklin?"

"Really? You're choosing now to bring that up? What was I meant to do, Scottie? Once ISIL got hold of Davey he was already dead."

"No—no, he wasn't." It took Wes a moment to notice because of the anesthetized quality of his speech, but Scottie was crying as he spoke. "We could've gone after him. We had the capability, and with the Kurds . . . We could've gone after him."

"No, we couldn't. And I'll tell you something, calling in that air strike wasn't easy, but it was a hell of a lot easier than risking seeing a video of them cutting off Davey's head."

Wes hadn't known Davey that well until he had moved down to Mardin. Even then, he'd left Davey to do his own thing—traveling down to Erbil every couple of weeks, working his own leads with the Kurds. But he'd come to know and like Davey Franklin in those fourteen months, and so had Rachel.

Davey had even talked once, over drinks, about what he'd want to happen if he ever fell into enemy hands. So, in truth, calling in the air strike *had* been easy, from a command point of view, because what Wes had just said was true and Davey had known it himself. He'd been dead the second he'd been taken, and in those circumstances, Wes's only responsibility had been to make sure it happened as quickly and painlessly as possible, for Davey, for his family, for the ongoing success of the mission.

What hadn't been easy was understanding how a smart operator like Davey had allowed himself to be taken in the first place. It was only seven or eight months later, in prison and with time on his hands, that Wes had thought back to Davey's final call from Erbil, the veiled suggestion that he'd learned something serious about the team. At the time, Wes had assumed he'd meant someone had been targeted, and in a way he'd been right about that.

"We could've gone after him," said Scottie one last time, without conviction. But his voice was stronger when he spoke again. "That was the turning point for most of us. That was when we switched from admiring you for getting results to seeing what a cold-hearted psycho you really are."

"Then you were wrong."

"No, we weren't. I know you're gonna kill me, because that's what you do, but I won't allow you to explain it away in your head, to convince yourself you're the good guy here and we're the bad ones."

"I'm gonna kill you because you murdered my wife."

"*You* murdered your wife! Think about it. Why was she trying to clear your name? Because deep down she knew you were a psycho, but she'd had your kid and she was terrified he'd end up nuts like you. That's all it was. She was desperate for some proof that you weren't as bad as she knew you were. Like I said, Wes, I did her a favor, just like you did Davey a favor. I saved her from the truth of who you are." He waited a beat and added, "Shame I didn't kill the kid too."

Wes shook his head. "I'm disappointed in you, Scottie. You think you can make me angry so I'll lose it and kill you quickly. But that's not how I am, you know that."

Scottie didn't respond. Maybe none of it mattered. Scottie would be dead soon, taking all his misconceptions with him. But Wes still felt the need to open his eyes on one matter.

"Davey called me the day before he left Erbil. I knew he was heading toward the front at Mosul and it didn't concern me—he was the best person in my entire team, and I include myself in that. But he also told me that we needed a conversation when he got back, about a serious security breach in the team, something he'd heard about from his Kurdish contacts. I never could understand how Davey fell into ISIL's hands so easily, and then I got taken down by being fed false information, and suddenly it all made sense."

"No." Scottie shook his head. "I don't believe you. You're trying to justify what you did, that's all, trying to pin the blame on someone else."

"It's a little late for that, don't you think?"

Wes got to his feet.

Scottie looked at him grimly. "Torture me all you like. You know I won't talk."

Wes stood on Scottie's ankle, pinning down the foot that still had a sneaker on it.

"I know that." He shot him in the shin. Even with the silencer, the noise was loud enough that the cicadas seemed to quieten briefly before the restless buzzing washed back over them. Scottie didn't make a sound but he was breathing hard, grimacing through the pain. "But I made a kind of implicit promise to Hamdi Berrada." Wes shifted his foot, standing with his full weight now on the entry wound. And this time Scottie let out a stifled squeal. Wes eased off. "Those poor people. You didn't just murder a boy who was simple, gullible, you didn't just trash his reputation, you destroyed the lives of his entire family, as well as all the other innocent people you killed, all to cover up the crimes of someone so rotten that even I was fooled for a while."

Through clenched teeth, Scottie said, "Collateral damage. You taught me everything I know about it."

Wes nodded, put his weight back on, moved his foot left and right, grinding Scottie's wound into the ground, and this time Scottie screamed, loud enough that people would have heard if there'd been anyone within a mile.

Wes waited until his cry fell away into a whimper, and said, "If you don't know the difference between collateral damage and cold-blooded murder, I didn't teach you nearly enough."

He stepped away, then moved backward another couple of paces and lowered himself against the tree. Scottie's head had collapsed against his chest, and with his cuffed hands in front of him, he looked to be in prayer.

"Scottie." He didn't lift his head. "Scottie, I need you to deliver a message to Sam Garvey for me."

That did the trick. He raised his head and stared at Wes in confusion, perhaps even hope, and with satisfaction, Wes reasoned that was a kind of torture in itself.

"I don't understand. What message?"

"Just this." He shot him in the chest, and this time the noise of the gun caused no ripple across the evening chorus, as if the violence had now been accepted and incorporated.

# Thirty

Wes watched Scottie die. He hadn't expected any pleasure or satisfaction from killing him and didn't feel any. It hadn't really been about revenge. Despite what he'd said to Scottie, he hadn't even really killed him for what he'd done to Rachel. He'd killed him because it seemed an appropriate response and, above all, because it was expedient—Wes had become a target of Sam Garvey's gray team, and Wes didn't like being a target.

This shallow hill was nothing like the barren one he remembered in Georgia with its rocky outcrops, but he was reminded of it even so, maybe just by the act of sitting on the unyielding ground beneath him. He thought of that day and wondered how his life might have been different if he had not detonated the bomb.

The mission wouldn't have been deemed a complete failure, but it wouldn't have been a success, not then at any rate, and Wes wouldn't have started his rapid rise to the top. Maybe Sam would have overtaken him and, in so doing, Wes might never have been set up, Rachel might never have been murdered, Wes would never have met Patrice, or Mia, who was waiting patiently for him back in the city.

He had no way of knowing how things would have turned out. The only thing he knew was that the little girl, whose name he still couldn't remember, would probably still be alive. She'd have been a young woman now, at university or finding her way in the adult world. It drove home the pointlessness of the whole thing.

And in some way, that only underlined the pointlessness of his own current position. He'd had little choice but to kill Scottie, but what good had it done him? He was no nearer finding Sam Garvey, so no nearer saving himself, no nearer finding Ethan. Ethan didn't even feel real to him as he sat there, and as Grace Burns had suggested, maybe that was the whole point, the reason Rachel had spirited him away in the first place.

Wes climbed to his feet, careful not to put too much pressure on his ankle, even though it felt fine now. He took the handcuffs from Scottie's wrists, then turned and headed back through the gathering darkness, trying to remember the way he'd come and where he'd left the car.

He'd been walking a few minutes when he saw lights. At first he thought they were a long way off, maybe even a car rounding a bend on the distant road, but then he realized they were much closer. The lights stopped moving and Wes headed toward them, not because he was curious, but because he was pretty certain this second vehicle had stopped behind the Lexus.

A man's voice called out in Spanish, questioning. Wes stopped moving, knowing that the man, whoever he was, would be listening for a response. After a few seconds he started to edge forward again, grateful now for the chorus of cicadas covering any sound his approach made.

The man had turned his own engine off, but his lights were illuminating the back of the Lexus, including the open trunk. It was hard to make out any detail from this distance in the rapidly hardening dark, but it looked like an SUV of some sort. Wes guessed it was probably the farmer who owned the land and, briefly, he wondered what sort of farming it might be.

The man moved in front of the headlights and Wes could see his silhouette bending and looking into the trunk, then moving forward and peering in through the open driver's door. He stood upright, looked into the night, maybe even right at Wes, and called out again, a single word.

Wes stopped walking once more, and moved again only when the man started back toward his own vehicle. And it wasn't until Wes was twenty yards short that the disturbing reality became visible. It was an SUV, but it wasn't a farmer, it was a police car.

The police officer had gone back to his radio now and was talking to his control. Even with almost no Spanish, Wes could tell that he was reading off the license plate on Scottie's car.

He waited in silence then, and Wes waited with him, working through his options. The worst scenario was that Grace and Noah had managed to free themselves and called it in, and that Grace's Agency colleagues had notified the Spanish police.

Wes guessed he'd know soon enough if that had happened, because the police officer would ask for backup and wait here until it arrived. Which wasn't an option for Wes. He'd have to kill him and get away before any more officers got here. But then he'd be a cop killer, and the Agency would make sure his picture and details were widely distributed with that real-world crime hanging over him.

The only other option would be to set off on foot, but even if he knew where he was going, it would take him at least a couple of hours to walk into the city, by which time the Agency would have tracked down Wes and Mia's hotel. And that meant she'd get dragged into it, too, which was the last thing he wanted.

The police officer got a response, he answered, and ended the call. He switched on a flashlight and moved back to the Lexus, studying the trunk, the interior. He found the gym bag and looked through that, then turned and slowly swept the light across the tree line.

Wes stepped back, conscious the tree in front of him wasn't big enough to shield him completely, but knowing that the distance between them, and the sheer expanse of country, would make it hard for the cop to spot him. The light rippled past, and sure enough, continued on its way in a futile sweep.

The police officer switched off the flashlight but still stood, as if listening to the landscape rather than watching it. Was he waiting for backup? Wes thought of Scottie's body propped against a tree somewhere behind him. He could shoot the cop, leave the gun in Scottie's hand . . . No, he wasn't thinking straight. The only smart option was to get back by foot, maybe reach a bar or suburb where he could call a cab.

And then at last the police officer moved again. He walked forward and closed the driver's door of the Lexus. He tried to close the trunk then but it wouldn't shut, and Wes wondered if Scottie had damaged the mechanism in opening it from the inside. He tried a second time and a third and the trunk finally clunked shut.

The officer got into his SUV, turned on the engine, sat idling for a little while. Another minute crept by like that before he finally turned it around and headed back down the narrow track.

Wes still waited where he was, listening to the cicadas, thinking again of Scottie somewhere behind him, praying at the foot of his tree, attracting various insects and other night creatures. Wes didn't know what this land was used for, so nor did he know how long it would be before the body was found or what would be left of it.

The police SUV made the road again and turned, not back toward the city, but heading in the other direction. For a while Wes could see the lights arcing this way and that, and for a while longer he could hear the engine growing fainter with distance.

Once he was certain, he got in the Lexus, turned it around, and headed back the way he'd come. He was less sure of the way in the dark, but after a while he started to pick up the signs to the city center.

It wasn't yet midnight when he dropped the car in a quiet residential street and walked back to the hotel, with the city becoming livelier as he got closer. He was sorry they'd have to leave, that she would not get the chance to visit the cathedral, but now that he'd broken cover, he knew there would be no slack.

He headed directly to Mia's room and knocked. He sensed her looking through the spyhole at him, then she opened the door. She had a look about her as if she'd been sitting in readiness for the last few hours—she was even wearing her sneakers. But she didn't seem aggrieved or put out in any way.

"Will we go now?"

"Yes." He stepped into the room and closed the door. "We'll tell them we have to drive to Málaga for an early meeting."

Her eyes lit up. "We're going to Málaga?"

"No, that's what we'll tell them. We'll head north, I guess." He looked at her, thinking of her father, wishing again that he'd taken the time to get to know him, thinking of the way he'd desperately tried to protect his daughter with his various pieces of advice. "Mia, after what I've done tonight, things could get worse. They might not, if I stay a step ahead of them, but I don't know what will happen. I think your father would have advised you to leave me somewhere and go home."

She smiled, as if to suggest that Wes had learned nothing. "My father always said to me—Mia, if you look inside, you will always know what is the right thing to do."

He didn't need to ask what she thought the right thing was on this occasion.

"Okay, but we do have to leave."

169

"Where will we go?"

"I don't know." He tried to think of something positive to say, but could think of nothing. He'd killed Scottie, used up his only leads, run out of forward momentum. "I just don't know."

And finally she looked concerned and Wes understood why. It wasn't because of the possible danger, but because Wes had been giving her a direction since stumbling out of those woods, and it alarmed her to see him lost.

# Thirty-One

They drove northeast out of the city. Wes took the tablet from the glove compartment and opened the Gmail account Raphael had given him. The email with the embassy staff list had come from another Gmail account, but Wes had no way of knowing if Raphael used it regularly—it was perfectly in keeping with Raphael's approach to security that he'd use it once to contact Wes and would never use it again. But it wasn't as if Wes had any other choices right now.

He sent an email asking Raphael if he could find the location of a CIA officer called Sam Garvey. Wes guessed the two remaining members of his old team were still with Garvey, so he added their names as additional options—Billy Tavares and Kyle Dexter.

Wes had never thought much of Kyle Dexter, and had wondered a few times how he'd managed to get through training, let alone survive in the field. He always needed someone else to tell him what to do, and then followed them blindly. So it wasn't too difficult to picture Kyle being swept up by Sam's narrative.

It was harder to accept that Billy Tavares had bailed on Wes. Billy was the only Native American Wes had ever met in the Agency, an Arapaho from Wyoming—smart, cynical, a shrewd operator, someone who'd covered Wes's back so often it was hard to imagine him betraying his former boss now. But he guessed it depended on what Billy had been told.

He put the tablet away and looked at the road for a while. Mia was driving with her usual casual confidence. She'd seemed disconcerted by Wes's lack of direction, but there were no signs of unease now.

"I guess we shouldn't drive too far tonight. It's late."

She pointed at one of the signs. "Sigüenza. It's close. There's a *parador* there. And a cathedral."

"You've been before?"

She laughed. "No."

He'd hardly left her alone since telling her that they had to leave, certainly not long enough for her to research nearby cities, their cathedrals and hotels. He could only imagine that she walked around with all of this information in her head.

"Well, let's hope the *parador* has rooms free."

"Yes, but there will be other hotels too, I think. And in the morning I can go to the cathedral, or will we need to leave immediately?"

"No, you'll have time to visit the cathedral."

He was about to remind her again that she didn't need to leave anywhere, run anywhere, but he knew what her response would be. And as long as they kept moving regularly, it would be hard for anyone to track them.

It was a little over an hour later that they reached Sigüenza. The *parador* did have rooms and the receptionist appeared unfazed by their arrival unannounced in the early hours of the morning.

They turned in immediately, but Wes sat for a little while watching the news, then struggled to sleep as his mind kept turning over what his next move might be. He wasn't off the grid—and wasn't sure he had the stamina to go off the grid—so even if they kept moving constantly, he wouldn't be able to stay ahead of Sam forever.

And Sam wouldn't give up. Ironically, by killing Pine and his two colleagues and by killing Scottie, Wes would have only made Sam more insecure and therefore more determined. Up until this point, Sam had been worried about his own past being exposed, but Scottie's death would have removed any doubt that Wes intended to neutralize the threat completely.

The only trouble was, unless Wes could find out where Sam was based now, he wouldn't be in much of a position to neutralize anything. He'd be operating blind, knowing the whole time that Sam would be using all the resources at his disposal to close in on Wes instead.

Eventually he drifted off and slept well for a few hours. He was woken by people chatting loudly as they walked past his room and was surprised when he checked the time and saw it was just before nine—he felt so rested that he was convinced he'd slept longer.

He'd finished breakfast and was lingering over coffee when Mia came in. He could tell from the air of peace about her that she'd already been to the cathedral. He envied her that outlet.

"Good morning, Mia."

"Good morning, Wes." She sat down opposite him. "Where will we go today?"

"I don't know." A little of her contentment crumbled away at the edges and he felt bad for that and tried to put a more positive spin on being so lost. "I guess if we keep heading north for now . . . I need some information, and until I get it I won't know where I need to go next. But it won't be Spain, so north is good."

"Barcelona?"

He shook his head. "Probably best for us to stay out of the big cities for now. We can head in that direction maybe, toward the French border, but stay away from the big places." In an attempt to give her some of the focus she so clearly wanted from him, he added, "Maybe if we drive on some of the smaller backroads we can find some villages with nice churches."

She smiled, either at the image or at the sense of purpose.

"Sigüenza is very nice. It's quite small, but it has a cathedral. I think today will be very hot." He nodded, unsure what other response he could offer. "Is the information about your son?"

"No, I . . . I'm not sure how I'm gonna find him. And maybe it's not a good idea for me to find him just yet, not until I know they won't kill me. The information I'm waiting for—it's about the man who got me sent to prison, the man who's trying to kill me. I need to find out where he is."

"So you can kill him."

"I guess so. It's the only way."

"The lady yesterday said you weren't meant to find him. The lady you shot in the leg."

"Yeah, I know the one you mean."

"She said you weren't meant to find him, that your ex-wife hid him from you."

He'd assumed she was talking about Sam Garvey but realized now that she'd gone back to talking about Ethan.

"That might be true. And what do you think? He's my son. His mother died."

"My mother died. I think a child needs a mother or a father."

"And your dad, he brought you up okay, didn't he?"

Maybe a lot of people would have questioned that, seeing the way she was, the problems she'd had and overcome. But Wes got the feeling Mia had been born different, and to the best of his abilities, her father had equipped her to live in the world.

Mia, anyway, was under no doubt. "He was a wonderful father."

And Wes took some consolation from that. He understood all too well why Rachel had wanted to hide Ethan away, but if General Nikola Pavić, convicted war criminal, could be a wonderful father, then maybe so could James Wesley.

174

# Thirty-Two

When they got to the car, Wes found his bible sitting on the passenger seat. He picked it up without comment and, once they were on their way, he opened it. She'd moved the bookmark again, to a chapter in John's Gospel, the anointing of feet and the procession of Jesus into Jerusalem.

Wes scanned through it looking for underlined passages, but as if summing up his own current uncertainty, Patrice had left only one notation, a question mark in the margin alongside a line of text: *He that loveth his life shall lose it; and he that hateth his life in this world shall keep it unto life eternal.*

Wes understood the confusion, because Patrice—or at least the Patrice he'd known—loved life with a vengeance. His question mark was probably asking why he should have to hate his life in this world to gain paradise in the next. Wes didn't feel strongly enough about his own life to be on either side of the fence—it was what it was, devoid of all love or hate, beyond hope or damnation.

He put the book aside and looked out at the road. Sigüenza was small and they'd already left it behind. Mia had taken his instructions on board and for the next hour or so they drove through increasingly remote country, avoiding the major roads, encountering no large towns or cities.

It was nearly lunchtime when they saw a village or small town perched on a hill ahead of them. A church tower stood tall at the top of it.

"Shall we go there?"

"Sure, why not? Maybe there'll be a restaurant. We could get lunch, maybe even stay the night if there's a hotel."

The landscape was dotted with trees, similar to the shallow hillside on which he'd killed Scottie Peters the previous evening. And yet, in some strange way, it reminded him instead of the country around Mardin, where he'd once been happy. It was surprisingly empty, and timeless too. There were some wind turbines on a distant ridge, and they alone offered any hint of modernity.

A smaller road branched off the one they'd been traveling, and even though there was no signpost, Mia turned off and drove along it, the SUV's suspension tested for the first time since she'd picked him up. They saw no other cars, no signs of agriculture or industry.

The village, too, seemed quiet as they passed the first houses. She slowed down, until at last they reached the small square and the church at the top of the little hill.

They got out, and Wes immediately knew that the village didn't look abandoned, it *was* abandoned. Now that he looked, some of the houses were in a state of disrepair, but they were all shuttered up, like vacation homes awaiting another season that would not come.

There wasn't a sound, and not even a breeze cutting through the handful of narrow streets. The baked intensity of the air felt like reason enough for the inhabitants to have given up and moved on. It seemed fitting somehow, a desolate village matching Wes's mood, his loss of purpose.

Mia approached the church door and tried it but found it locked. She started to walk around the building and he fell in with her. They walked a little way through the adjoining streets before giving up and heading back to the car. It was so hard to believe that an entire village could have died that Wes still looked from side to side, expecting some sign, a single house still occupied, a person scurrying away along one of the narrow streets.

They took to the road again, but the thought of the abandoned village nagged at him, its loneliness unsettling. If it bothered Mia she showed no signs of it. Her concentration was entirely on the road, as if the village had been possessed of no more meaning than that they had not been able to eat or find a bed for the night, that she had not been able to visit the church.

After another couple of hours the landscape shifted again, more forested now, more temperate. As they came over a small crest in the road they could see what looked like another hilltop village ahead of them.

"Shall we go there?"

It appeared to be directly in their path anyway.

"Sure."

He was actually thinking that this landscape was no less remote than the place where they'd stopped, and that this village would probably be no less abandoned, but as if reading his thoughts, she smiled and said, "This one is different."

"I'll take it on trust."

Once they were down off the crest and among the trees they lost sight of the village, but Wes also sensed that it was no longer in their path, that the road was taking them away from it.

They reached a turning and this time there was a sign, albeit faded and in need of repair. The words "Monasterio de Santiago" were faintly visible but nothing else. Mia turned without hesitation and Wes guessed there was no reason not to—it wasn't as if they were in a rush to get anywhere else.

With that thought in mind, he checked the Gmail account, but there was nothing. He put the tablet back in the glove compartment and looked across at Mia. She was smiling a little, maybe simply because the buildings they'd seen were a monastery rather than a village.

"You understand it's probably deserted?"

"No, I have faith."

He shrugged, smiling too—if she still had faith after seeing that sign maybe she was onto something. They drove for fifteen minutes, but this road, even though it was narrow, seemed well maintained, and Wes began to think her faith might not be completely misplaced.

They started to climb and immediately took a sharp right-hand bend and found the walls of the monastery rising up in front of them, the gates open onto what looked like a lush and bright interior. To the left of the gates was a gravel parking lot, home to a dozen upmarket cars.

She parked and turned off the engine, and Wes said, "Well, I was wrong about that. And either these are some really wealthy monks or this is a hotel."

She smiled back at him. "No one will find you here."

"That's true. I guess we can stay a couple of days, if they have room. Maybe by then I'll know what to do next."

Even as he said it, though, he started to worry he was riding his luck. Until now, Mia had provided cover for him, but Grace and her boyfriend had seen her, knew her name was Mia. It wouldn't take too many lucky guesses to identify her and put a trace on her credit cards.

They walked through the gates, seeing for the first time a small brass plaque—*Hotel Monasterio de Santiago*. A door opened into a reception area and a young man came out of a back office to greet them.

Even as the man was welcoming them, Mia interrupted him, saying, "Do you have a chapel here?"

He took a moment to regroup, then smiled. "Of course. For weddings?"

"She just likes to visit churches. Do you have two rooms for a couple of nights?"

"I see. Yes, I'm sure we can do that."

"Great. And do you mind if we pay in cash up front? We've kind of maxed out our cards and I've still got all this to use before I fly home." Wes held out the bundle of banknotes he still hadn't touched since Bordeaux.

Mia stared at him quizzically, as if he were performing some kind of street magic.

"Of course, as long as you have ID."

"Naturally."

The receptionist smiled and said, "And I apologize for the mistake about weddings. I misunderstood."

"No apology needed. It'd be a great place for a wedding. It's beautiful."

"We like to think so."

In fact its beauty turned out to be completely at odds with what Wes had expected to find here after visiting the abandoned village. Within its walls was a large garden of flower beds and fruit trees, with a restaurant area and bar on one side, a pool on the other.

And there was peace there. The other guests seemed to lounge reading by the pool, or sit quietly over dinner. There was no disturbance in the hushed, cool corridors. If the monks had returned it might have taken them a little while to see that it was no longer a religious house.

There was safety too, Wes was certain of that, and yet he couldn't relax, knowing that he wasn't moving toward any of his goals either. He checked the Gmail account a dozen times and was beginning to give up on Raphael getting back to him.

Mia asked him if she could do anything to help and so the next afternoon he handed her the envelope with the contents of Rachel's room safe from Granada.

"Why don't you take a look through that—see if you can find any clues."

"You think your son might be in there?"

"Maybe. Maybe Sam Garvey too, the man who wants to kill me. My wife was investigating him, so there might be some clue. You might see something I missed."

Given the way her mind worked, he was surprised at himself for not having asked her to look through the various pieces of paperwork before. Every time he looked there were too many reminders of Rachel, too many triggers, whereas Mia would focus on the task at hand.

So they sat for most of the afternoon in the dappled shade of the fruit trees near the bar. Wes was simply killing time. He dozed, he walked around the gardens a couple of times, he sat looking across at the two couples by the pool, one elderly, the other consisting of an older and grossly overweight man and a trim glamorous woman in her thirties.

Meanwhile, Mia studied the contents of the envelope, paying meticulous attention to every receipt, every ticket. Once she'd finished most of it she picked up the pile of postcards she'd put to one side.

"It's okay? To read these?"

"Sure. Like I said, she just wrote notes on them. She never sent them."

Mia nodded, looked at the picture on the first, then turned it over and frowned with concentration as she read the handwriting on the other side. For the next twenty minutes she studied one after another, occasionally smiling, even laughing, at the things Rachel had written.

He'd read a few of the cards himself and hadn't spotted any-thing particularly funny, and he wondered if that was just another sign that he'd never really understood her, or if it was just Mia's skewed take on life, finding amusement where there was none. He didn't ask her now what was tickling her, not wanting the answer to his own question.

When she finished, she shaped all the cards neatly into a stack and put them in front of her on the table. She looked satisfied, as if she'd just read a particularly enjoyable novel.

Wes had just picked up the tablet yet again, and smiled at her before turning back to the screen in front of him. He accessed the Gmail account and was so used to seeing it empty that it took him a moment to see that there was a new email there, from the same account.

He opened it, his heart kicking up a beat, then sinking again as he saw Raphael's words.

*I'm sorry, man, I've tried everything and I can't find Sam Garvey anywhere. He's really well hidden . . .*

"Is it bad news?"

He glanced at her, nodded. "Maybe."

But then he looked back to the email and laughed as he read on, not so much at the contents but at the location.

*. . . but I had more luck with the other two. Even with them, I can't find an address, but I can tell you with 98% certainty, they're in . . .*

Wes smiled now. "Maybe it's not bad news after all. I think it's time for you to go home, Mia."

Her own responsive smile faltered. "I don't understand."

"Zagreb. Here we are in Spain, but the people I'm looking for have been in Zagreb all along."

"Really? The man who wants to kill you?"

"His colleagues are there, and I'm pretty sure that means he's there too. How about that? Zagreb."

It made sense. He knew there'd long been talk of putting a gray team in the Balkans. George Frater had vetoed it more than once, but clearly the new guy in charge, Aaron Schalk, had been persuaded otherwise.

"So we can scatter my father's ashes."

"Yes, we can." He liked the fact that she'd included him in that. "And maybe you can help me find the people who want to kill me."

"Yes, I can do that. I know people. In Zagreb. We leave in the morning?"

"I think so."

"I can book a very nice hotel."

He could see that she'd absorbed a lot of his own doubt and uncertainty since leaving Madrid but was now feeding off his renewed purpose. He could see her enthusiasm flooding back.

"Don't you have a house in Zagreb?"

"Of course. It's where I'll scatter my father's ashes. I'll never sell it. But I won't stay there again, not ever."

He thought he understood, but didn't want her to dwell on it, so he pointed and said, "You didn't find anything?"

"No." She looked down at the postcards, then picked the stack up and went through them before pulling one aside. "Except this."

He looked across at it, unsure what she was getting at. All he could see was a picture of a cathedral, pretty much interchangeable with all the others.

"What about it?"

"It's not in Spain. It's in Italy."

He reached out and took it from her. He turned it over and read the small printed caption—it was the Duomo in Milan. He hadn't noticed the message before either; not so much the content—*For old times' sake!*—but the writing itself. It was similar to Rachel's handwriting, but it wasn't hers.

Alina had been Rachel's witness at their wedding, her oldest friend from college. And Alina had been Milanese. He thought of the train receipt that had no corresponding ticket. Had she traveled to some meeting point—maybe Barcelona—and handed Ethan over to her oldest friend? Had Alina brought the postcard, remembering Rachel's odd habit from the many shared travels of their youth? And had Rachel kept the postcard in the hope that Wes might . . . No. That was a speculation too far, but the underlying truth was harder to doubt.

"My son is in Milan."

"You're sure?" He nodded, still looking at the picture of the Duomo, trying to think of alternative explanations, nervous of investing in this hope, but knowing he had to be right. "So we should go to Milan first?"

Yes, more than anything, he wanted to go to Milan, but he couldn't do that, to Rachel or to Ethan, not until he knew it was safe. And it would never be safe until he'd dealt with Sam.

"No. Zagreb first. Then Milan."

"But your little boy is safe? You know the person he's with?"

"Yes, he's safe for now. He's with someone who was at my wedding."

And there was some bitter irony that the principals in Wes's hasty and short-lived marriage were all reunited here in some fashion. Rachel's maid of honor had naturally been the person she'd turned to when she'd needed to guarantee the safety of her child. While Wes's best man had effectively brought about the end of the marriage, killed Rachel, and was still determined on killing Wes. If a person's friends were the measure of them, it just seemed to offer one more piece of proof that Wes had never been nearly good enough for her.

# Thirty-Three

They left early the next morning. He didn't ask Mia why she'd chosen the feeding of the four thousand in St. Mark's Gospel for him to read, but he understood well enough why Patrice had underlined a particular passage near the end of it—*For what shall it profit a man, if he shall gain the whole world, and lose his own soul? Or what shall a man give in exchange for his soul?*

It was a question Wes could quite easily put to Sam Garvey and the others who'd betrayed him. But he didn't plan to be asking many questions, not now.

They made the coast north of Barcelona and more or less kept to it as they crossed southern France. They stopped for lunch outside Montpellier and stayed the night in Menton near the Italian border.

When they set off the next day he was given Isaiah for company. But again, he was more intrigued by Patrice's choice of underlined passages, because this one seemed particularly appropriate in the light of Wes's journey—*Say to them that are of a fearful heart, be strong, fear not: behold, your God will come with vengeance, even God with a recompence; he will come and save you. Then the eyes of the blind shall be opened, and the ears of the deaf shall be unstopped.*

"That's something else," Wes said, and turned to her. "What makes you choose the things for me to read?"

"The black man." She threw a quick glance before turning back to the road. "I think he must be a very wise man. He chooses very interesting things."

Wes smiled. It had never occurred to him that she'd always intended him to read the sections underlined by Patrice, that she'd also been intrigued by them.

"He is wise."

"His name is Patrice."

"That's correct."

He looked across and could see her smiling to herself as she concentrated on the road.

They crossed the north of Italy and stayed that night in Trieste. But the next morning Mia seemed preoccupied and he noticed the bible had been left where he'd placed it on the back seat. He picked it up anyway, and was oddly disappointed to find the bookmark still on Isaiah. Idly, he tugged at the other bookmark, easing the blade clear of the spine before sliding it back in. It felt like an age since he'd driven that spike into Skip's neck.

They drove across a narrow section of Slovenia, and as they approached the border and the traffic began to slow, Mia said, "Croatia is in the European Union, but not in Schengen. So. We have to go through customs."

"Will they search the car?"

She looked at him with a dismissive smile. She'd been so out of sorts since breakfast that it was a relief, but he also wondered if she understood that he was carrying a serious amount of weaponry and ammunition.

"Why would they search?"

"I don't know, maybe . . ."

He didn't know. When they got to the Croatian customs post, she handed in the two passports. The border guard looked at Wes's first and frowned and looked across at him with what appeared to be suspicion. He said something and Mia replied—the first time Wes had heard her speak in her own language. The border guard looked unimpressed by her response, but he casually opened her passport and Wes noticed his demeanor change instantly. He asked Mia another question, she answered to the affirmative, and the border guard reacted as if to a celebrity, offering warm words, waving them through, even nodding respectfully to Wes.

Once they were driving again, Wes said, "He recognized your name?"

"Yes. Many Croatians are called Pavić, but he knew who I am when he saw it. Some people do. Some people don't."

That was the end of it, and she fell back into silence. They reached the coast again, the Adriatic this time, but then turned inland at Rijeka. And now, as they drove through the forested hills of her country, the unease she'd seemed to exhibit turned to something more like a nervous excitement and she started to talk.

"It's a beautiful country, don't you think?"

"Yeah, I guess so."

"When I first saw Renaissance paintings, you know the religious paintings, in Italy, I thought they were all painted here, because the countryside in the background, it looked like Croatia, in every one. It was very exciting for me, as a child, to see that."

"Because you were religious?"

"Of course. Many people in Croatia are religious. Young people like me." It was the first time he'd heard her refer to herself as a young person. "I'm twenty-nine. I don't really remember the war. Or my mother." She smiled, and appeared to almost breathe in the landscape. "It was a very happy childhood for me."

He wasn't sure what to say in response. She'd grown up without a mother, she'd developed an eating disorder and a problem with self-harming, was possibly autistic, and yet her belief in this happy past seemed genuine. Wes's childhood had been about as safe and stable as it was possible to be and yet all he really remembered was how bored he'd been most of the time.

"So you must be happy to be back."

Her smile turned into a frown of concentration.

"I don't know. Thinking of happy times can make people sad—isn't that so? I'm coming to scatter his ashes. It's what he wanted. And then . . ." She fell silent briefly, apparently unable to think past the scattering of her father's ashes, but then her face brightened a little. "And you must kill some people."

"I don't have to kill them, I just . . . Actually, no, you're right—I do have to kill them. I won't be able to get my son otherwise. And anyway, they wanna kill me."

"Because they're afraid of you, like the people in Madrid."

"Yeah, I think so. They betrayed me, and they think I'll want vengeance, so they're trying to kill me first."

"Which is why you have to kill them."

"Yeah." She laughed, presumably at the circularity of it all.

She continued to talk on and off, of nothing in particular, and then as they reached the outskirts of Zagreb she started pointing out places and landmarks, sometimes talking about memories of her past.

Then as they neared the center she said, "The hotel is called the Esplanade. It was built for passengers from the Orient Express—you know, like the novel?"

"Yeah, I know the one you mean."

She pointed. "There it is."

It was an imposing block a hundred yards from the station, and she drove up the sloped entrance to the front doors as if it were something she'd done a hundred times before. Maybe she had, because there seemed to be a mix of familiarity and respect from the three young men who emerged from the hotel—one taking the bags, another the car keys, the third standing by the door and offering a welcome to them in Croatian.

Mia replied, just a few words, and the young man turned to Wes with a bow and said, "Welcome to the Hotel Esplanade. I hope you'll enjoy your stay in Zagreb."

"Thanks, I hope so too."

He showed them inside and handed them over to one of the people on the reception desks. As they were invited to sit, Wes noticed the same deference. Mia was in her typical attire—sneakers, tight black jeans, a black long-sleeved top—yet there was something almost regal in the easy manner with which she accepted this special treatment.

As the woman behind the desk handed the keys over, she said in English, "We've upgraded you to a suite, Miss Pavić, and you too, Mr. Wesley, so that you can be nearby."

He nodded. It was clear from her tone and expression that she thought he was a bodyguard or some other employee.

In the elevator, Mia said, "How will you find the people you must kill?"

"I'm not sure. I need to find out if anyone's aware of an office being run somewhere in Zagreb by Americans, something that seems suspicious. I know that's a bit generalized."

She shook her head. "It's a small city. People will know, and I know people who will be able to find out."

"Good, but first, I think we need to do something else."

She stared at him for a few seconds, a puzzled expression, and said finally, "You want me to guess?"

"No, I . . ." Even now it took him by surprise that normal conversation was so full of riddles for Mia. "I just mean, we should scatter your father's ashes."

"Oh, yes. But your business is urgent."

188

He didn't want to have to explain to her that his business might make it hard for him to be involved in the scattering of her father's ashes. Even if Garvey hadn't secured backup from the Agency, there were still at least three of them and Wes didn't see many ways of it ending without him killing them all—or getting killed by them in the process. No matter how many friends Mia had in Zagreb, he'd probably need to leave immediately after it was done.

"You've waited long enough, and so has your father. I think we should do it now, this afternoon."

She stared at him again for a few seconds, but he knew she understood this time. Maybe her real reluctance was founded in simply not wanting to say a final goodbye.

# Thirty-Four

They drove across the city and then up into the surrounding hills, along a leafy road with large houses set behind electric gates. She told him that rich people and many foreign ambassadors lived here. She slowed down then as they approached a gate set in a wall that seemed to have only woods beyond it. The gate was open and an elderly man was standing next to it—he waved as Mia drove in.

"Did he know you were coming?"

"Yes, I telephoned. He looks after the house. He has an apartment, in the basement, with his wife."

She headed up the drive without slowing, beyond the woods to the nineteenth-century mansion that sat amid immaculately maintained lawns. The house itself looked closed up, shutters blocking the windows on the upper floors.

As they got out of the car, the caretaker was strolling toward them. He and Mia had a brief conversation, the old man making the sign of cross and shaking his head sadly as he walked away.

Wes looked up at the house and said, "You grew up here?"

"Yes. It was wonderful to be a child here."

He noticed the caretaker had disappeared around the side of the house, rather than climbing the steps to open the main doors.

"But you don't want to look inside?"

She shook her head. "The house is full of happy memories."

He understood her point, even as he wondered if General Pavić had seen it that way. Mia walked to the back of the car and took out the cardboard box. She opened that and removed the functional-looking urn that contained her father.

"There's a tree near the back of the house. My father liked to have a chair there. He would sit and read or sleep in the summer. I think that would be a good place."

"Show the way."

He followed her around the house and across the lawn. There was no chair beneath the tree now, but a small patch of grass looked a little worn, presumably from the General resting his feet there over many years. It would grow back eventually, but was still in evidence even after the years Pavić had spent in prison.

Mia stood and bowed her head. For a little while she seemed deep in prayer, then she unscrewed the top of the urn and scattered the ashes around the base of the tree, as if feeding it. The air was still and already warm and the ash rested where it fell, a gray scar against the green of the lawn.

Once she'd finished, she put the top back on the urn and placed it on the ground next to her. She bowed her head again and this time as she prayed he noticed her lips moving slightly. When she looked up again she smiled at him but there were tears streaming down her cheeks.

Wes took a Kleenex from his pocket and held it out, and as she took it off him, their fingers touched, the most fleeting of contacts. But even now, even after all the time they'd spent together driving across Europe, her hand recoiled as if she'd touched something hot. He imagined some people would have been hurt by that response, but he only pitied her, imagining the storm that had to be raging in her head that she could be so disturbed by the touch of another human.

She dried her eyes and said, "Thank you for coming. It meant a lot."

"I was glad to be here." He looked down at the ashes, looking like powdered cement on the grass.

"We can go now. You can kill the people you need to kill."

"I have to find them first."

"Yes."

By the time they got back to the car, the caretaker was waiting again. Another short conversation ensued, and as they drove away, Wes noticed the caretaker ambling down the drive to close the gates after them.

"Tomorrow I will go to the cathedral."

He looked across at her, though she was focused on the road.

"You've been before, I guess."

"Many times. But I can go to Mass. You can come too, if you like."

"No, I'll leave that to you."

She smiled, as if at some private joke, or maybe just at Wes's unwillingness to visit a cathedral.

Back at the Esplanade, the concierge spoke to Mia in Croatian as soon as she walked into the lobby. She answered, thanked him, then turned to Wes.

"I have visitors waiting for me in the bar. Perhaps they will be friends of my father. So they could help."

He nodded and they walked through to the bar together. There were maybe ten people in there, but Wes noticed three gray-haired men sitting around a table—they were probably about the same age as General Pavić, and although they were all portly now, they had a military bearing about them.

As soon as they saw Mia, they stood, and as she neared them they bowed. Wes wasn't sure if that was the customary polite greeting anyway or if they knew—as everyone from her past surely did—about her dislike of physical contact. She introduced Wes in English and they all shook his hand.

One of the men called the waiter over and ordered more drinks, and Mia said to Wes, "These men were colleagues of my father. They fought together in the war. I've known them my whole life. We'll drink pear brandy with them now."

"Okay."

Wes noticed the one in conversation with the waiter was a bull of a man, huge across the shoulders and with a thick neck and his hair cropped as if he were still in the military. Despite their age, all three of them looked robust.

The waiter was treating them with what appeared genuine respect, smiling and laughing with the big man. The other bar staff were looking on from across the room, also smiling, seemingly pleased to have these men here, and like Mia, none of them looked old enough to remember the war.

It cheered Wes in some way, maybe just to see a country that still respected its heroes as well as its celebrities. Wes hadn't fought for anything as momentous as a country's independence, but he'd fought to maintain America's security, and he couldn't help feeling a hint of bitterness at the treatment that had been sanctioned against him.

Two more glasses were brought, together with the bottle of pear brandy, which the waiter left on the table once he'd poured the two new measures and topped up the other three glasses.

The big man raised his drink and said something, and Mia turned to Wes. "We're toasting my father."

"I'll drink to that."

He joined them and they drank. The pear brandy was just as explosive as he'd expected it to be, but he followed them in draining it and watched as one of the men filled the five glasses again. Wes hoped they wouldn't be making many more toasts.

"Is it okay if we speak in Croatian?"

"Sure, go ahead."

He presumed from the tone of the conversation that followed that she was talking to them about her father's final days. They listened respectfully, nodding, occasionally upset. One of the men said something that Mia disapproved of and her measured rebuke was enough for him to offer a fulsome apology and the big man to pat him reassuringly on the shoulder.

Everyone sipped at the glasses of pear brandy, which were once again filled. Then the big man gestured to the waiter. Wes hoped he wasn't ordering more drinks—his tolerance for alcohol was still a long way from returning to its pre-prison levels.

There was a brief exchange with the waiter, and he came back quickly with a sheet of paper and a pen. The big man thanked him and placed the paper and pen on the table in front of Wes.

"Please. Write down the names of the three men you need to find. They're not in the embassy?"

"No." Wes was certain Raphael would have found them if they'd been attached to the embassy, and the whole point of the gray teams was that they weren't answerable to an embassy or station. "But they'll have an office in the city, probably dressed up as a shipping agency or something like that."

"It's a small city. Leave it with me."

Mia smiled and said, "Uncle Slavko will find them." Then she added, "He isn't really my uncle. I have two uncles but I don't see them. Uncle Slavko is better than an uncle."

As big as he was, Slavko suddenly looked boyishly embarrassed by the compliment and said something under his breath in Croatian, a tone of modesty about it.

"Well, I appreciate your help. It's possible there are more than three, but I don't think it will be many more. But it's important for you to know that these are dangerous people. They'll be expecting

194

me to come to Zagreb, but it's best they don't know I'm already here, and . . ." He was about to suggest Slavko shouldn't engage with them himself, but Wes could see how advice like that would probably be seen as a challenge. It wasn't even as if he was worried about Slavko's safety, so he simply fell back on the truth. "These people, they got me sent to prison, and they arranged the murder of my wife. I'm sure you'll understand, I want to deal with them myself."

"I understand. We'll find out where they are, and then it's up to you. But if you need help, of course, we are here. What Mia asks, we give."

Wes nodded, seeing the truth in that, but it was something that played on his mind after they left, and also later over dinner in the restaurant. Mia was a well-known figure here in Zagreb. Grace Burns and her friend Noah would have reported back that Wes was traveling with someone very distinctive-looking. They hadn't heard her surname, and without it the puzzle might be harder to piece together.

But it wouldn't be impossible, and Sam Garvey had apparently outwitted Wes once before. No, they wouldn't know that Wes was here yet, and they wouldn't know Mia was with him, but given her renown, it might only be a matter of time. Things were okay for now, he was confident of that, but he hoped Slavko could come up with something quickly, because Wes was certain he wouldn't be the only person searching for someone.

# Thirty-Five

Mia went to the cathedral the next morning. Wes slept soundly, probably helped along by the pear brandy and the wine at dinner. He had breakfast out on the terrace that overlooked the square and the railway station beyond. There was a strong breeze, but when it paused he could tell that it would be warmer than the previous day.

He lingered over breakfast, thinking she'd come and join him as she had on other occasions following her cathedral visits, but she didn't come. He remembered then that this was not just a visit, that she was attending a service, so in the end he walked back through to the concierge desk.

"Good morning, sir!"

"Good morning. I wonder, have you seen Miss Pavić come back?"

It seemed like an extraordinary request given the size of the hotel and the number of people coming and going in the lobby, but aside from Mia's social standing, her startling appearance made her hard to miss.

"I saw her leave, but I don't think she's returned yet. I saw her talking to Josip at the door before she left. Perhaps you could ask him."

He pointed to the bald middle-aged man standing on duty in front of the main doors.

"Thanks." Wes walked out and asked the same question.

"No, sir, not yet." He checked his watch and produced the slightest frown. "She was going to morning Mass but that would finish before ten. Maybe she went shopping?"

It was ten thirty, so there wasn't much in it, particularly now that she was back in her own city, a place full of landmarks and meaning for her. But Wes couldn't fight the beginnings of a creeping nausea in his stomach. Just last night he'd considered and temporarily dismissed the possibility of Sam targeting Mia, but it was back in the forefront of his mind now.

"Did she walk?"

"Of course, sir. As you can see, a beautiful day."

"How far is it?"

"About ten or fifteen minutes in that direction, but if you'll excuse me, it's pointless you going to intercept her—she could take any route back to the hotel." With a hint of curiosity, maybe even suspicion, Josip said, "Don't you have her cellphone number?"

Wes knew there was no true answer he could give that wouldn't lead to outright suspicion—he didn't have a cellphone because he'd just been released from prison and someone had tried to murder him; he didn't have her number because they hadn't really been apart since he'd come bloodied out of a French forest; more than that, he didn't have her number because they didn't really know each other at all.

"She doesn't take her cellphone when she's going to church."

"Of course, I should have thought of that. She's very religious, like many young people in Croatia." Josip didn't have much more to offer. "I'll tell her you were looking for her. When she comes back."

"Okay, thanks."

Wes walked back into the hotel. The concierge was busy talking to another guest so he slipped past unnoticed and went upstairs.

He rang the bell to her suite, just in case she'd come back without them noticing. Getting no answer, he returned to his own room.

He looked out of the window, down at the terrace below where they were just clearing away after breakfast, out at the square with people walking and cycling, trams and cars moving in a continual clockwork motion, taxis sitting outside the station.

Everything looked normal about this early summer day. And it was perfectly normal for a twenty-nine-year-old woman to go to church and take her time coming back. But that nausea was still there, and it wasn't just the fear that something might have happened to her, but also that he had indeed been outmaneuvered by Sam Garvey yet again, and with relative ease.

He waited an hour, and was just beginning to think it might be worth walking to the cathedral anyway when the room phone rang.

"Good morning, Mr. Wesley, you have a visitor—he's waiting in the bar for you."

"Thanks, I'll be right down."

He imagined it was probably Slavko and hoped he'd already come good on his promise to track down Garvey's office. At the same time, he hoped Slavko didn't ask where Mia was, because although it was too soon to presume she was missing, Wes didn't trust his own unease not to show through.

When he got there the bar was a little busier than the previous day. Wes scanned the faces—he was looking for Slavko and was surprised not to see him there. Then something pulled his gaze to the far corner of the room, where a man in a plaid shirt was sitting on his own. His hair was short and reddish-brown and he was sporting a suspiciously hipster-looking beard.

He didn't wave when Wes looked in his direction, but their eyes met. Wes walked toward him but he did another quick survey of the bar as he moved across it, checking who else was in there.

Wes's caution was well founded, because the beard was new, and looked faintly ridiculous, but the man was Sam Garvey.

And now Wes was angry, at Sam but also at himself. He'd told her time and again to leave him, and he'd accepted her refusals because he was weak, because he'd needed the company and liked being around her. But this was what his weakness had led her to, a dire situation summed up in the smug face of Sam Garvey.

As he got there, Sam smiled and held out his hand.

Wes looked at it but left it hanging as he sat down. Sam raised his eyebrows, as if to say there was no need for bad manners, and let the hand drop again.

"I was hoping we might be able to sort things out, Wes, but you don't seem to be in a very conciliatory mood."

Wes didn't answer because the same waiter from the previous day came over and said, "Good morning, Mr. Wesley, what can I get for you?"

"The same as yesterday, I think. Thanks."

"Of course."

The waiter looked expectantly at Sam.

"I'll have the same as him."

"Coming right up."

The waiter left and Wes said, "Almost didn't recognize you with the facial hair."

Sam stroked the beard, smiling. "Just keeping up with fashion, you know."

"No, I don't. I've been in prison for three years. What do you want, Sam?"

"You're the one who came looking for me. What do *you* want?"

What did he want? He wanted Ethan, he wanted Rachel not to be dead, but beyond that?

"Honestly? I don't know. I've been thinking a lot about it, all that stuff about emotional intelligence. See, I know what I think I should want, but I don't feel it. It's nothing so primal as revenge, it's just expediency, or like a mental exercise, a war game—these are the problems, what are the most logical solutions. What do I actually want—that's a tough question."

"Jesus! Have you *any* idea how insane you sound?"

The waiter came, carrying a tray. He placed the two small glasses in front of them and poured from the bottle of pear brandy.

"Should I leave the bottle, like yesterday?"

"Yeah, thanks." Wes picked up his glass as the waiter took the tray away. He looked at Sam. "How about a toast?" Sam cautiously raised his glass and Wes said, "To Rachel."

He drank the shot back in one and, reluctantly, so did Sam. Wes filled the glasses again.

"Where were we? You were telling me I sound insane. I don't think I am, but one thing I do know is I'm not stupid—that's your specialty." Sam raised his eyebrows again—maybe he'd always had that tic but Wes hadn't noticed it so much without the beard. "All you had to do was visit me twice a year while I was in prison, keep lying to my face—you were good at that—and I wouldn't have suspected a thing, and your man Pine could have killed me so easily. All the complexity of your crimes and your treason, and yet you undermine it with one stupid oversight. It was always your problem, the reason you had to rely on treachery to get me out of the way, because you were *never that smart*."

Sam smiled, but it was pinched, and he sighed, as if unsure where to start.

"I certainly haven't come here to defend myself against you, Wes. Maybe in your own mind that's how you think it was, that I was corrupt, that I had to get you out of the way, that I was afraid Rachel would find out the truth so I had to kill her. The fact is, you caused all this. You were out of control, running things like it was your own little fiefdom, sharing more information with Konstantin

Grishko than you were with Langley or even your own team. You'd become a liability."

"I was getting results."

"In appalling ways, using appalling methods."

"Seriously? *You're* taking the high ground on *my* methods? You tricked a kid into becoming a suicide bomber and used him to kill a dozen people, just to stop Rachel getting to the truth."

"I did no such thing." He looked angry and sipped at his drink but put it down again, a sour expression on his face. His tone was earnest when he spoke again. "You know how gray teams work. I gave Scottie a job, but without rules of engagement. I had no idea he'd kill all those innocent people. I did instruct him to kill Rachel, and that was the hardest decision I've ever come to in my life, but I couldn't allow her to get to Grishko. The collusion between you and the GRU, there's just no way we could allow that to get out, not in the current climate."

How things had changed, how easily cooperation had become collusion, how quickly a diplomatic and strategic success had become something that needed to be buried.

"Why didn't you just kill Grishko? You killed him anyway."

"It was too late for that. Grishko would've offered confirmation, but she'd already dug too deep. And she thought she was clearing your name, but my God, she was close to learning things about you that would not . . . Well, the only consolation is that she never got to that."

Sam was the second person to suggest this, that Rachel had been spared unpalatable truths about Wes by being murdered. Maybe she'd have discovered details she wouldn't have wanted to know—he'd had to do things in the Middle East that might have weighed heavily on some consciences—but there was some irony in Sam suggesting that death was better than the truth.

"You think she didn't know the kind of person I am, the kind of things I've done? She worked out of my office for nearly two years. Even if she didn't know the details, she knew. And instead of trying to deflect things onto me, how about we concentrate on the important truths. Grishko and I both knew that someone in my team was working with Omar Shadid, working against our interests, even jeopardizing our missions. When Davey Franklin started to suspect you, you betrayed him, made sure he fell into ISIL's hands." Until now, Wes's explanation for what had happened to Davey had been only a theory, but Sam's blank expression convinced Wes he'd been right about it all along. "But even that wasn't enough. You thought I was close to finding out, so you set me up for a fall, too. Took my job, took my team. And then Rachel made the mistake of looking into my past, trying to clear my name. So you killed her, you sent your team to kill me, and then you killed the only other person who could've exposed your dealings with Shadid—Konstantin Grishko."

Sam leaned forward and forced himself to take another sip of his drink. Wes downed his in one, and filled his glass again.

"Are you done? It's a great story, Wes—"

"I'm gonna kill you, Sam. I guess it's because of what you did to me and what you did to Rachel, but ultimately, it's because I still think of myself as an Agency employee, as a servant of the US government, and there's no doubt in my mind that killing you would be a great service to my country."

"No, Wes, you aim to kill me because it's what you do. It's your default option. But that's not how this plays out. I'm sure you've deduced by now that we have the girl. And really, you accuse me of being stupid, but you waltz into a small city like Zagreb with a high-profile companion and check into this place, and you didn't think we'd notice."

That stung because it was true, but Wes didn't let it show, smiling instead.

"The 'stupid' thing really got under your skin, didn't it, Sam? Because it's true, and you know it. You're acting like you're in control, but you're not. It's why I climbed the greasy pole ahead of you, and why it took a scheming traitor like you to bring me down."

"Maybe I am stupid. Maybe that's why it took me so long to realize you're completely nuts, but enough of the reminiscing. Be in your room tonight at ten. You'll get a phone call and you'll have thirty minutes to get to the rendezvous. If you're not in your room when we call, or if you don't reach the rendezvous, we'll kill the girl, slowly."

Wes laughed a little, then more, a response that appeared to crack the surface of Sam's confidence.

"That's your bait? You think after all I've been through, I'm gonna walk into an ambush and get killed just to save her? You paint me as inhuman, yet you still think I'll commit suicide to save a woman I hardly know? No. I don't care what you do with her. And you really do seem to be having trouble understanding, so I'll make it plain. I. Am going. To kill you."

It was true, Sam wasn't the smartest, but he was smart enough. After staring back at Wes for a few seconds, calculating, he relaxed, even produced a smile, then stood up.

"Ten tonight. One way or another, this plays out the same. You can do it the easy way and save the girl, or the hard way and she dies. Your choice."

He walked away quickly. Wes waited a few seconds, then jumped up and followed, calling over to the waiter, "Charge it to my room—I'll sign later."

"No problem, Mr. Wesley. Have a good day."

Wes smiled back, because that was exactly what he planned to do.

# Thirty-Six

By the time Wes got to the main doors, Sam had already crossed the street and was walking away to the left, talking into his cell. Wes watched him walk, struck by his confidence, by the fact that he didn't once look back.

"Everything okay, sir?"

"Everything's fine, thanks, Josip."

Despite Wes's jokes about him being dumb, Sam wasn't dumb enough to walk away so casually, not unless someone was covering his back. Wes looked around but saw no one. He ducked back in through the doors but moved so that he could stare back out, looking over Josip's shoulder.

He was there for a full ten minutes before he spotted someone walking out of a small café across the street and heading in the opposite direction to that Sam had taken. Even then, Wes had registered the movement and almost dismissed it before he realized it was Billy Tavares.

Billy had already turned the corner and disappeared from view by the time Wes stepped out and pointed, saying to Josip, "Where does that street lead to?"

"To the shopping district and up to the old town."

"Okay, thanks."

Wes broke into a run to get across in front of an approaching tram, then kept running until he was on the same street as Billy, a tree-lined avenue of what appeared to be grand apartment blocks. He slowed to a walk once he caught sight of Billy up ahead of him.

Billy Tavares was an imposing presence and looked every bit the Native American. In Turkey and Iraq he'd been able to blend in easily enough, but in a predominantly white city like Zagreb he was an all-too-visible target, so Wes was confident of keeping him in sight now that he had eyes on him.

But Wes wasn't sure what he planned to do. He didn't have a gun on him. He'd momentarily considered going back to his room to get one, but Billy would have been long gone by then.

On the other hand, Billy *would* be armed and was no push-over even without a weapon. At the very least, Wes could find out where he was going, make a note of the address, and head back there later—not that he had an abundance of time in which to act.

For the next ten minutes, he followed Billy, the street more or less a straight line so that Wes was able to keep his distance. He closed in more tightly as they hit a pedestrianized stretch and the shopping district—there were a lot more people about now so it would be easier for Wes to lose him, and harder for Billy to notice a familiar face behind him.

Billy cut into a passage and then climbed some steps up into a small tiered park built into the hillside. It looked like a hangout for students and artists—deck chairs here and there among the trees, someone in a hammock, a table tennis game in progress, a small bar.

Billy disappeared from view, and as Wes reached the top of the steps he saw that he'd walked into a pedestrian tunnel, the outside painted like a cartoon monster, its open mouth forming the entrance. It appeared to cut right under the hill that made up the old town, but it was long and straight and Billy was the only person in it, clearly visible as he walked away, so Wes had no choice but to hold back.

He only followed when he thought he might be in danger of losing him, but even now he was conscious that Billy could turn at any moment and Wes would be an easy target against the light of the tunnel entrance. Would he shoot him here? Wes guessed it depended how much they'd all fallen for the portrayal of their former boss as some kind of dangerous maniac.

Billy turned right up ahead, so Wes picked up his pace, and as he got nearer to the junction he could hear voices, echoes of conversation and laughter, footsteps on the stone floor. He rounded the corner into a larger tunnel and he could no longer see Billy at all.

There were stalls set up here selling jewelry and crafts; another that appeared to be some kind of art installation, two women fitting people with VR headsets. Wes threaded through them, picking up his pace again. There were more people ahead of him—a young couple, a small group of teens—and by the time he got through them, the tunnel ahead was empty, right up to the point where it broke back into the light.

Wes ran on. Did Billy know he was being followed? He'd covered this distance pretty quickly for someone just walking home, but then he'd had a decent head start. Wes only slowed again as he emerged from the tunnel, back into the full glare of the sun.

He turned left, reckoning Billy wouldn't have come all this way to double back on himself, and he was proved right—there he was, a short distance ahead, not looking rushed. For the first time, Wes wondered if Billy wasn't heading home or back to the office, but to wherever it was they had Mia.

He closed in again as they walked along another busier street. They passed alongside a restaurant that had tables out on the street, full of couples and groups, a mix of tourists and locals. Wes spotted a steak knife sitting next to a plate, and as he walked past he let his hand brush the edge of the table and took the knife with him—no one seemed to notice him taking it, but as he slid it inside his sleeve he also wasn't sure how much use it would be.

A couple of minutes later, Billy stepped into an old apartment building. The street door was open, and as Wes approached, he could hear Billy's light footsteps on the stone stairs. Wes moved quickly, noiselessly ascending, pulling the knife free from his shirt sleeve, an action that inevitably reminded him of releasing the blade from Patrice's bible.

Billy's steps were still above him, but Wes could tell he was gaining on him. And then the noise stopped and so did Wes. He glanced up. There was no sign of Billy, so he was somewhere on the third floor. Wes moved again, reaching the landing, a quick step forward and a glance to left and right. Billy wasn't there.

Wes moved forward again, looked left, took in the deep doorways that opened into each of the once-grand apartments. He started to turn back to his right but instinctively sensed someone stepping out behind him, and he was annoyed with himself for not seeing him there, for being outwitted.

But he had to channel that anger. Even without looking he knew Billy would have a gun, and that he was maybe only ten feet away. Without even thinking about it, without even turning to make sure it was Billy behind him, he hurled himself back, colliding with him, crunching him into the wall.

He'd closed the space down before Billy had raised his gun arm, but he knew the gun was drawn as it cracked hard against the top of his head. A fist slammed into his torso on the other side then the gun arm got withdrawn, and Wes knew Billy was pulling it back just enough to take aim so he punched back hard with his right arm, three times, Billy's arm smashing against the corner of the doorway until the gun clattered to the floor.

Wes rammed the same hand down then, a fierce blow with the knife into Billy's leg, and used the shock of that injury to spin around. He took a punch at Billy's face with his left and immediately brought the knife up and pushed the tip under his chin, and both of them became still.

Wes's heart was racing, he was out of breath, his head and his ribs already beginning to throb. Billy was out of breath, too, and his lip was bloodied. He looked afraid. Wes had seen Billy Tavares go into some dangerous situations over the years, and he'd never seen him look so scared before.

"Which is your apartment?"

Billy gestured with his eyes to the door behind him.

"Anyone else in there?"

"No."

"Turn around. Face the door, hands up where I can see them."

He eased the pressure of the knife but kept it at neck level and Billy made a hobbled turn, struggling to put pressure on the stabbed leg. Wes took a quick look to the left, saw the gun on the floor a few feet away. He had the knife pressed into the back of Billy's neck now, the sweet spot just under the skull.

"Where's the key?"

"Right-hand pocket of my pants."

Wes kept the knife firm and reached his hand into the pocket, pulling the key free and slipping it into Billy's hand where it was pressed against the door. He stood back then, and in one swift movement stepped away, scooped up the gun, and aimed it.

"Okay, open the door."

For a second, Billy didn't move, and his reluctance was visible even as he grudgingly slid the key into the lock. He'd moved from fear to grim realization, but Wes was pretty certain he could at least rely on him not to beg.

Once the door was open, Wes pushed the gun into Billy's back and moved inside with him, closing the door shut again with his boot. They moved around the apartment like that, like some fraught modern-dance routine, until Wes was certain there was no one else there.

The bathroom was the last stop and Wes opened the cabinet and found a first-aid kit. He handed it to Billy, who for the first time showed another expression—confusion.

"Through to the living room." Wes walked behind Billy, and now that he was more relaxed, he noticed how tidy it was, how spare. "Take off your shoes and your pants, then sit on the couch there and fix your leg."

Billy stared at him groggily. He kicked off his shoes, loosened his pants, easing the bloodstained material away from the wound and then dropping them. He sat and looked down at the wound as he opened the first-aid box.

"Doesn't look too bad," said Wes.

"It went into my quad pretty deep. Lucky, I guess."

He didn't sound as if he meant it, and Wes was pretty sure he understood why. Billy thought this was a bluff on Wes's part, to make his victim think he didn't plan to kill him, to get him to talk.

"I'm not gonna kill you, Billy."

Naturally, he didn't look convinced, and grimaced as he wiped the wound with disinfectant.

"Is that what you told Scottie?"

"Have they found him?"

"Yesterday." He looked up briefly, then went back to patching up his leg. "And you didn't answer my question."

"Scottie killed my wife. I feel like you all betrayed me, too, but frankly I'm not bitter enough about that to kill you. Scottie killed my wife. Sam ordered it. There's no need for it to go beyond that."

"I never betrayed you, Wes. I do the job I'm told to do, so did Scottie. I liked working for you—you were a good boss, but you went to prison."

"Sam seems to think I was out of control."

"I don't hold with that. You were in control. You were extreme, but that was the nature of where we were. It needed someone who didn't believe in taking prisoners."

"Was I extreme?"

Billy looked up. "Permission to speak candidly?"

"Granted."

Billy still looked reluctant to talk, a hesitancy that for the first time made Wes uneasy about what he was going to hear.

"Yeah, you were extreme, everyone thought so. The Kurds loved that about you, the fact that you were always willing to do whatever it took. The thing is, you were scary to be around sometimes, in the field, but in a weird way I always felt safe, because you were on our side, not theirs."

For a second or two, Wes could think of no response, because he still didn't recognize Billy's depiction of him, or not all of it.

In the end, he said, "Thanks for being honest."

"I'm sorry, Wes. I meant no criticism. We need people like you, we—"

"It's okay, Billy, I understand. And so I guess that's why you think I'm gonna kill you?" Billy looked back at him but didn't answer. "It's not about taking no prisoners for me, but I'll admit, it's about always doing what needs to be done. If I needed to kill you, I would. You could argue it's a risk for me to leave you alive, but I'm willing to take that risk. You're a good man, Billy. I thought Sam and Scottie were too, but I was wrong about them."

"They—"

Wes silenced him with a raised finger, because he didn't want to hear another defense of either man. "Where have they taken the girl?"

"I don't know. I wouldn't tell you if I did, but Sam has this philosophy of separate cells. He'd have told Kyle and Brandon to pick her up and keep her somewhere but then he'd have just left them to it. As of now, not even Sam will know where they've got her."

That squared with what Sam had said about telling Scottie to shut Rachel down but not how to do it. It was a smart way for a traitor to operate, ensuring there was no thread running through the maze.

"You have an office here in Zagreb?" Billy shook his head, not a denial but a refusal. "This is between me and Sam. How about an address? Let me go in there on even terms."

"I can't. You know I can't." There was an air of resignation about him—even if he'd accepted that Wes didn't intend to kill him, he looked like a man who was expecting to be tortured. And he was right in a sense, because if Wes thought it would do any good, he'd have tortured Billy to the outer edges of death. But he knew Billy was too strong, that it would take too long.

Wes thought of a line from the bible and was amazed that he could remember it—maybe some of it had been sinking in after all.

"Greater love hath no man than this, that he lay down his life for his friends."

"What?"

"Something a friend of mine underlined in a bible he gave me. I guess it fits. I don't know if you consider Sam a friend, or even a comrade, but you certainly know you're risking your life to protect him."

Billy nodded. "I know that. And yeah, I consider him a friend. I consider you one too."

211

"You remember Omar Shadid?"

"It's probably my only regret out there, that we didn't take that cockroach down before we left."

"Sam was working for him." He nodded in response to Billy's incredulous expression. "We knew someone was, but didn't know who. I think Davey Franklin had his suspicions—that did for him. Sam set me up. I guess he was worried I was getting close to the truth. That's certainly why he killed Rachel. And why he killed Konstantin Grishko."

"Grishko's dead?"

"A week or so after Rachel. She was on her way to meet him when she was killed. So when you come to your debrief, I want you to tell them what I've told you. I want you to tell them that Pine and his colleagues tried to kill me and I killed them in self-defense. Tell them I killed Scottie because of what he did to my wife. I didn't kill Grace Burns or her boyfriend, and I didn't kill you."

"You're really not gonna kill me?"

"It's not my plan, but you have a choice here, Billy. If you trust me—and think about it, I really have no reason to lie at this stage—then turn off your cellphone, take some painkillers for that leg, and lie low for the night. If I see you again tonight, I'll have no choice, because I'll have to assume you trust Sam more than me, and that you're my enemy. You understand?"

"I understand."

"Good. Who's Brandon?"

"He joined the team eighteen months ago when we moved here. He's okay."

"Kyle, Brandon, Sam. Any more?"

Billy didn't answer, but Wes was sure that would be it—gray teams were meant to be tight-knit, even if Wes's had unraveled anyway.

Wes stood. "He plans to call me tonight at ten with a rendezvous point, so that's all you have to do, lie low until ten, let us sort it out between ourselves."

"You know what'll happen if you show up to any rendezvous?"

"I know." He pointed. "Sorry about the leg."

Billy shrugged, an admission that it had been a more or less fair fight, no apology needed, and maybe also an acknowledgment that a wounded leg was nowhere near as bad as this might have turned out for him.

# Thirty-Seven

The sky overhead was blue, but he could see ominous clouds stacking up on the horizon and the heat was building to the kind of sticky intensity that suggested a storm was overdue.

He found a dumpster at the back of a café and dropped the gun and the knife into it. He walked on for another five minutes, but with the humidity and the throbbing in his ribs and on his head where Billy had cracked him with the gun, he was in no mood to walk all the way back to the hotel. He picked up a cab to take him the rest of the way and when the driver tried to explain that it wasn't far to walk, Wes simply told him he was in a hurry, which was true enough.

Back at the Esplanade he walked up to the concierge's desk and said, "One of the generals I met with Miss Pavić yesterday, I don't remember his surname, but his first name is Slavko."

"Of course, General Novak."

"Great, so, I need to get hold of him."

"But he's here now. He arrived twenty minutes ago. I thought you were expecting him."

"We were, kind of. I didn't realize he'd get here so soon. Er, where is he?"

"In the bar."

"Thanks."

Wes walked through and found the bar quieter now that most of the lunchtime crowd had gone. Slavko was sitting on his own, staring at his phone as if still trying to work out how to use it. Wes could see the familiar bottle and a glass on the table in front of him.

The barman caught Wes's eye and held up a small shot glass questioningly. Wes nodded, smiling—it seemed he was becoming "the pear brandy guy."

Slavko looked up as Wes approached. He looked a little surprised, probably to see Wes on his own. Wes noticed the brightly colored cartoon graphics on Slavko's phone and Slavko looked down at it himself and laughed.

"My grandson, he likes me to play this game. We compare scores. It's a crazy game but I'm quite good at it now. He doesn't always win." He put the phone away and shook Wes's hand as he sat. "Where is Mia?"

It was just simple curiosity. The best-case scenario if Wes told him the truth was that he'd have a whole bunch of allies in his battle against Sam. The worst-case was that Slavko would be furious at Wes for putting Mia in danger in the first place, and he'd have been right to feel like that. Nor did Wes know how it would play out tonight, so for now it was better Slavko didn't know.

"I think she's visiting her favorite haunts, places she remembers. She went to a service at the cathedral and I guess she's doing some shopping, you know, that kind of thing."

That seemed to satisfy him. The waiter placed the glass on the table and poured a shot from the bottle, then topped up Slavko's glass. They drank and then Slavko reached into his jacket and pulled out a piece of paper which he placed on the table between them.

"Your friend has an office not far from here. The company is called Holdfast Shipping, but my information is that this is just a front. Three of the people who work there have apartments in the city, two you named and another, Brandon Myers. The other man you named, Sam Garvey, he isn't listed as a resident anywhere. But . . . the office of Holdfast Shipping is on the third floor of the building. Above it on the top floor is an apartment, also owned by the same company, but no resident listed. So I think you find him there."

"Thanks. Would you happen to know who occupies the neighboring buildings?"

Slavko smiled.

"I thought you would ask this. On the left is a financial company. On the right is a magazine publisher and, on the top floors, a TV production company." Wes was about to speak but Slavko held up his finger, a gesture that was almost identical to the one Wes had used against Billy, but Slavko was still smiling, pleased with himself—and it seemed for good reason. "Also on the paper, you will find the entry code for the building on the right, and for the TV company offices. I imagine you want to get to the roof?"

"I really appreciate this. If there's ever anything I can do . . ."

"You were in prison with Nikola."

Had Mia told them that yesterday? He wondered if she'd been back in touch with Slavko since, and what she might have told him.

"I was, but I didn't know him very well. I think that was my loss."

"He was a great man." He frowned, the look of someone contemplating unresolved business of some sort. "And you and Mia, what is your connection?"

"When I got released from the prison, Sam Garvey sent three people to kill me. I killed them, but I was hurt. I came out of the woods and Mia just happened to be driving past. She rescued me, and she's stuck with me ever since. But I should stress, there's no . . ."

"Romance? You don't need to tell me that. She's not like other people."

"Yeah, I worked out that much. She's told me a little bit about her past, how her mother killed herself, how she doesn't really talk to her family anymore, but I'm not sure if that has anything to do with the way she is."

Slavko frowned again, but this time because he seemed to be struggling to understand what Wes was getting at. Then a light appeared to come on.

"Ah, I see. No, she was born this way. The problems with the family are connected. They would always tell Nikola she has autism or some other disorder, that he should seek medical advice. They said other things too, not so nice things. So Nikola cut them off. It didn't matter to him that she was different. He only wanted to make her happy, to help her live her own life."

Wes nodded his understanding, but wondered at the same time if seeking medical help might have prevented the period of self-harming and the eating disorder.

"As for her mother—she was a beautiful woman, but she suffered so badly in the war. She was very close to her brother, but he was killed, also her best friend. After Mia was born she had a depression, and in truth, she never recovered from it, and then when she lost her brother and her friend, it was all too much. This is a happy country now, Mr. Wesley, but there are ghosts."

"I understand."

Slavko brightened. "But it's good Mia has a friend. I worried when Nikola died, what she might do, but she found you. There's a reason for all these accidents. You believe that?"

"Honestly, I don't know." Wes picked up the piece of paper. "But I'm grateful for this."

"It's my pleasure."

He raised his glass and Wes followed suit and they drank. It had been Slavko's pleasure, but he probably wouldn't have felt that way if he'd known the truth, that Wes had been complacent or incompetent enough to put Mia in danger. And he guessed by the end of the day they'd all know just how valuable it was, and how dangerous, to have Wes as a friend.

# Thirty-Eight

The Holdfast Shipping office was in a monumental-looking block probably only a five- to ten-minute walk from the Esplanade, in the direction he'd seen Sam heading after their meeting. The facade was an imposing fin-de-siècle cliff face, but the roofs were pitched, with skylights facing both front and back.

Wes learned that much from the computer in the hotel's business center. Armed with this knowledge, he had a taxi take him to a hardware store and bought duct tape, a glass cutter, a flashlight, and cable ties—a shopping list that seemed inherently suspicious to Wes but didn't even earn a raised eyebrow from the young cashier.

Then he went back to the hotel and waited, but not for a phone call. He wouldn't be there when Sam called, and that was typical of how lacking Sam was in the cutting edge—it had never occurred to him what he'd do if Wes simply didn't play along. The one thing even Sam wouldn't want to do was kill Mia, not when she was their only leverage.

Just after eight Wes set off on foot under a sky of towering clouds, taking a route that meant he could approach the offices he wanted without passing Holdfast Shipping first. The TV production company was spread over the two upper floors and he walked around them, looking at the layout, getting a sense of what the neighboring property looked like.

He listened too, using a glass, and even though the walls were thick, he could hear occasional movements coming from the office next door and, just once, someone speaking on the phone. There was no noise coming through the wall from the apartment on the top floor.

He found a stepladder, and with half an hour to go and darkness finally falling, he climbed out through the skylight onto the roof. One thing he hadn't been able to see on Google Maps was quite how steeply pitched the roof was, and while the front had a decorative stone balustrade as part of the facade, the rear offered nothing more than a gutter to stop him falling if he slipped.

He edged forward but immediately felt himself sliding, and retreated to the skylight frame. So instead of going across, he used the purchase of the frame to push himself up the roof, high enough to reach the apex. He could hardly shimmy along the very top like a cartoon cat burglar, but using it as a handhold he was able to crab-walk along the roof until he was above the neighboring skylight.

The window frame stood proud of the roof so he was able to let go and slide down to it. A quick glance revealed a bathroom, in darkness, no light from beyond the closed door.

Even here, with few places from which he might be spotted by neighbors, Wes didn't want to hang around for long. He slipped his backpack off and got the duct tape and the glass cutter. He taped up the glass, folding a couple of lengths of the tape to make handles. Then he cut around the edges and used the handles to pull the sheet of glass free. He rested it flat on the roof, wedged against the top of the frame, put the tape and cutter back in the pack, then lowered himself through the gap and dropped lightly to the floor below.

He pulled his gun and waited, listening. Now that he was inside he was acutely conscious of the noise of the city coming through the open skylight, the traffic of a perfectly ordinary early-summer evening. He couldn't hear anything from within, not even when he stood against the bathroom door.

He took out the flashlight, eased the door open and moved through the apartment, checking each room, sticking close to the edges to avoid telltale creaking boards. It was evidently occupied, and in the bedroom Wes found a framed photo next to the bed, of two young girls. Sam had married young and divorced not long after the youngest girl had been born.

He studied the picture. He guessed the girls were about eight and ten now. It made him think in turn of Ethan, how Rachel had planned to ensure Wes would never have anything to do with him. If she hadn't been murdered, Wes might never have even found out about him. He wanted to be angry with her about that, but his certainties had been undermined enough by what Billy Tavares had told him that he no longer knew what to think.

He took a sharp knife from a block in the kitchen, slipped it into his pack, then left the apartment and made his way down the stairs. He'd feared there might be a coded door into the Holdfast office, but it followed the same layout as the TV production company, treating these two upper floors as one property, with a secure door offering access to both of them.

The office door had a glass panel in it, and Wes could see an empty reception desk beyond it. The overhead lights weren't on, but there was a subdued light coming from somewhere within. He pushed the door a touch, just to make sure it wasn't locked, then waited, looking at his watch as the minutes crept by.

On the hour, Wes pushed the door again and slid silently inside, easing it shut behind him. To the left of the reception area was a wall with three doors, all open onto darkened offices. To the right, beyond the reception desk, there was a lounge area with two low couches facing each other over a black glass coffee table.

The light was coming from an open office door beyond that lounge area. And Wes could also hear Sam's voice now, asking to be put through to Wes's room.

Wes moved closer as the call ended, then stood still and listened. His hearing was so acute in this silence that he could tell Sam had made another call because he could hear the ringtone coming from the receiver.

"Hey. He's not there. He didn't answer." Wes couldn't hear any indication of a response, but there clearly was one. "I don't know. I guess we move to Plan B. Any word from Billy?" This time Wes could hear the single-word reply from the other end and Sam seemed to pause before responding. "Okay, we have to assume the worst."

Wes was glad he'd judged Billy right on this one. Some people would have considered it desertion, abandoning his colleagues, but Wes saw it as nothing more than putting right a past wrong.

He stepped into the office. Sam was facing him across the desk and immediately started to reach for the drawer, but Wes shook his head and waved the gun at him.

Sam made a show of slowly lifting his hand clear and away from the drawer, and said into the phone, "I have to go, but move to Plan C. Plan C." He moved the other hand then, the same theatrically slow movements as he hung up the phone. Wes smiled, stepped closer, put the phone properly into its cradle.

"Same slow movements, open the drawer, take the gun out, put it on the desk."

He did as Wes told him, placing the holster on the desk. Wes leaned over, pulled the gun free of its holster and slipped it into his pocket.

"This is why you were never cut out to lead, Sam. What a crazy plan. I mean, seriously, it might work in some stupid movie, but in real life? I could've just disappeared and you would've spent the next ten years of your life looking over your shoulder."

"But you didn't," said Sam, a hint of triumph, as if he still wanted to believe he'd found Wes's weak spot by taking Mia. And he tried to hide his curiosity with an air of contempt as he added, "And how would you have done it better, if my plan was so bad?"

Wes thought about it, seeing the obvious solution. "I'd have planted a bomb under the car. That way, she would have looked like the target."

"So you're not so opposed to collateral damage after all."

He had a point, and if Rachel had been a target and not his wife, the suicide bombing in Granada might once have seemed to Wes a perfect solution. Maybe the only thing that had really changed was his employment status.

"I'll give you that. Now, let's move into the lounge."

"You know they'll kill her?"

"Really? Is that Plan B or Plan C?" Wes gestured with the gun again, making clear he didn't want an answer this time. Sam pushed himself away from the desk and walked out of the office in front of Wes. "Sit on the couch there, back to the door."

Once Sam was sitting, Wes dipped his hand into the bag and took out two cable ties and threw them onto the glass coffee table in front of him.

"One around your ankles, one around your wrists. And it's crucial for you not to make any unforced errors at this stage."

Wes leaned down and switched on the lamp next to the other couch, and then watched closely as Sam put the cable ties around his ankles and wrists, using his mouth to pull the one around his wrists tight. But Wes had seen the way Sam had left himself a little space with both.

"Lift your feet, put them on the table." Sam did as he said and Wes pointed the gun at him as he put one knee on top of Sam's legs

223

to stop him kicking out, then yanked the cable tie tighter around his ankles. "Raise your hands above your head." Sam pulled his feet back off the table and raised his hands. Wes walked behind the couch, grabbed Sam's wrists, and clicked the handcuffs in place.

Confident that Sam wasn't going anywhere, he went back and sat on the opposite couch, throwing his backpack to one side, taking the gun from his pocket and placing it on the couch, too. He saw Sam eyeing the gun where it sat camouflaged on the black sofa cushion, maybe imagining he might be in with a chance if he could get to it.

Seeing him trussed up, Wes wondered how he'd even got into a gray team, let alone become the leader of one.

Then, as the thought occurred to him, he said, "Why would we even need a gray team in the Balkans? I'm sure there's work to do out here, but not for a whole team. George Frater never saw the need, I know that much."

"Frater's history. I made a case for it. Schalk saw my logic."

"I still don't get it." And then he understood too well. "My God. Shadid. Omar Shadid wanted you here. The Balkans—the perfect gateway for trafficking people and drugs into Europe. Is that how much you're in his pocket?"

"I never worked with Shadid. It was never about that. It was about you becoming a danger, to your team, to your country."

"What's Plan C?"

"Plan C is a choice. You die or she does."

Wes nodded. He reached into his pack for the duct tape, got up, and walked behind Sam again. He could see Sam trying not to look at his own gun sitting on the other couch, could see him trying to build up the nerve to leap for it. In the end, he didn't. Wes tore off a long strip of tape and put it across Sam's mouth, smoothing it fast against the beard and pulling it tight around the back of his head.

He went back to his pack for the knife he'd removed from the kitchen upstairs, before returning once more to stand behind Sam. He slipped his gun into his belt, grabbed hold of Sam's hair and used the point of the knife to score a neat line up the back of his neck, midway between the carotid and the top of his spine.

But the knife wasn't quite as sharp as Wes had imagined. The point dragged a little as it tore the skin and drew blood. Sam produced a muffled cry and strained against the smarting touch of metal.

"You've probably heard of the death of a thousand cuts. I read about it in prison just the other week. I had a lot of time to read in prison. The Chinese actually called it the lingering death." He repeated the same cut on the other side of the neck, talking over the cry this time. "Believe it or not, it wasn't removed from their penal code until 1905. Expert executioners could take up to three days to kill the victim, slowly slicing apart their bodies, making sure to miss all the key arteries and organs. Of course, I don't have three days."

He put Sam in a headlock and stabbed the knife down into his shoulder. Sam buckled, fighting against it but at a disadvantage. Using Sam's own movements, Wes grabbed his arm, pulling it up so he could make a shallow piercing stab into the side of his abdomen. Sam creased over, not so much with pain this time, but with a desperate realization that this wound was worse.

By the time Wes moved back and sat on the couch again, there was already a dark patch blooming across Sam's shirt on the side of his stomach and a look in his eyes that was pleading, in spite of everything, in spite of all the things he'd done to Wes, all the things he believed about him.

They sat like that for a few more minutes, a stillness in the air around them. Sam was trying to stay calm, probably thinking it was his best chance of staying alive long enough for his remaining men to rescue him, and maybe there was some logic in that—despite the blood and the four wounds, he probably wouldn't bleed to death if they got treatment for him within the next half hour.

Wes heard a vehicle pull up somewhere, though it was impossible to tell whether it was at the front of the building or out back. He had his gun in his hand, his eyes trained on the door which was just in view beyond Sam's head. Another minute crept by and then he heard the clumsy footsteps of two people leading another up the stairs against her will.

They stopped at the top, then he heard them code in and the outer door opening. A prolonged pause followed. The office door pushed open a fraction and Kyle Dexter shouted through it.

"Wes, we're coming in! We've got the freak—you try anything and we kill her first, you get it?"

He felt his stomach tighten with anger at Dexter calling her a freak.

"Wes?"

"I get it."

"Okay. There's no reason we can't all walk out of this tonight, all go our separate ways, put it all behind us. Agreed?"

Wes slid Sam's gun along the couch and wedged it deep between the two cushions.

"Agreed."

"Okay, we're coming in."

Wes smiled at the increasingly enfeebled Sam Garvey. This was Plan C, and Dexter wasn't fooling anyone.

# Thirty-Nine

They pushed Mia through the door first. She tried to smile when she saw Wes sitting there on the other side of the room, but she was also fighting the distress of being manhandled. Dexter's hand was clamped around her arm just above the elbow, the other hand propelling her forward with the gun barrel pressed into her back.

In the same way that Billy Tavares had stood out on the streets of Zagreb, so Dexter had always stood out in the Middle East, with that Mormon missionary look that gave away his nationality. Wes had been with him in a small town in eastern Turkey once and the local kids had even pointed at him and shouted, "Jason Bourne! Jason Bourne!" He'd taken it as a compliment, not as proof that he was the least undercover person working for the Agency.

Now though, Dexter had grown a beard, just like his boss. But whereas Sam looked like a desperate guy approaching middle age and trying to keep up with the fashion, Dexter just looked like a confused geography teacher.

He stopped in the open doorway and said, "Put the gun on the table in front of you." Dexter's voice was shaky with nerves, probably because he'd found himself where he'd never expected to be—in charge.

"Why would I do that? You'll just kill me."

"I'll kill her if you don't." Wes still didn't move, and Dexter looked at the back of Sam's head. "Sam?"

"He's got duct tape over his mouth. He's hurt but he's still alive."

"What do you mean, 'hurt'?" His eyes flicked in Sam's direction, and the outraged expression suggested he'd seen the blood on his neck. "What did you do to him?"

"He's fine. Surface wounds."

Wes looked at Mia again. He didn't know if she was trying to communicate anything to him or if her mind was completely focused on the hand clamped onto her arm, but he thought of what she'd said about Grace Burns being scared of him, and he could see now that Dexter was full of fear. He was so full of fear he couldn't even see that he and Brandon Myers had the upper hand here—Dexter still desperately wanted someone to give him a way through the situation.

"Tell you what, Kyle, you give me your assurance, as a former colleague, that you won't shoot me, and I'll put the gun down, just so that we can talk through this and find a way out for everyone."

Dexter's eyes darted about, landing on Sam a few times, as if desperate for his current boss to explain what his former boss was doing.

"Okay, I'll give you my word. But you try anything, Wes, anything at all, and I'll kill her first, then I'll kill you."

"Deal."

Wes leaned forward and put the gun on the glass table. Sam had been staring blankly, a passive witness to Dexter's arrival, but now his eyes darted across to the couch as if looking for his own gun. It had apparently disappeared, but Sam knew it was still there somewhere and that Wes would use it.

Sam groaned something urgent through the duct tape but Dexter misunderstood and said, "Don't worry, boss, we'll get you out of there." Sam slumped with frustration in response.

Dexter pushed Mia right into the room now and she glanced down at the back of Sam's head, or at the bloodied neck, curious rather than horrified. For the first time, too, Brandon Myers came into view, stepping into the office and letting the door swing shut behind him.

He was late twenties, dark hair, average build, forgettable features—the right look to have had a decent career in this line of work. His gun was hanging casually at his side. His eyes were scanning the room. If he'd looked at Sam he'd have seen that Sam was still fixed on the couch and the spot where his gun had been until a moment before.

"Brandon, get the gun off the table there. Keep watching him. And Wes, remember what I said."

Wes nodded, and watched as Myers walked around the couch, leaned over to pick up the gun, then retreated, never taking his eyes off Wes, like someone in the presence of royalty. He put the gun on the reception desk and turned back to Dexter.

"Okay, get the duct tape off of Sam's face." Dexter craned his neck, looking over Sam's shoulder, then looked at Wes. "Where's the key for the cuffs?"

Wes pointed to the backpack. "Want me to get it?"

"Nice try. Toss the pack onto this couch." Wes threw the pack so it landed next to Sam. "Okay, duct tape first."

Myers holstered his gun and started working at the tape on the back of Sam's head, but as he pulled, Sam winced, then cried out through the gag.

"Sorry, boss." He worked more closely, slowly easing the tape free from Sam's hair, inching forward toward his beard.

Dexter watched him for a few seconds, then looked at Sam and smiled. He felt he had the upper hand now, just as he was about to lose it, mistaking Wes's patience for surrender—the moment the tape came off Sam's mouth, that would be the time, because Sam would start shouting and they'd be distracted.

But it was taking a long time, and Sam's eyes were watering with the pain of his hair being pulled up by the root with the tape. Wes couldn't help but note that they made pretty good duct tape here in Croatia.

Dexter's confidence seemed to be growing and he sneered a little at Wes and said, "So, how did you two meet? She one of these crazies who likes to visit prisoners?"

"You've no idea who she is, have you—whose daughter she is? Anything happens to her, your life's over."

Sam let out a little cry as Myers started to pull the tape off his cheeks.

"Sorry, boss."

Dexter looked at the ongoing operation to remove the duct tape, then back to Wes. "No, I don't know who she is and I don't care. What I do know is you didn't wait long after your wife died before picking up with someone else. I mean, I don't go for this graveyard chic myself, but whatever turns you on, I guess."

He let go of Mia's arm and raised his hand, and in slow motion Wes saw what he was about to do, and saw simultaneously that his own moment might come sooner than he'd expected. Dexter had been holding her over the sleeve of her sweatshirt, but now he reached up to stroke his fingers down her cheek, probably intending to be menacing, but with no concept of how dramatically she'd react when his skin touched hers.

Wes slid his hand along the couch, his fingers reaching down into the gap between the cushions, closing around the cold certainty of the gun.

At the same time, Dexter's hand reached Mia's face. Contact. Mia screamed. Wes had expected her to scream, but this was a yell of attack, of fury rather than fear. She lashed out, elbowing Dexter hard in the neck, spinning around and away from him, launching a kick.

Dexter hit back at her instinctively, knocking her off balance, and at the same time he leveled his gun at Wes. Myers let go of the duct tape, leaving it hanging from the side of Sam's face, and reached for his own gun.

They were both too late. Wes pulled Sam's gun free and fired twice as he raised his arm, the explosion of the shots tearing the room apart. One bullet hit Brandon Myers in the side, sending him pirouetting to the floor behind the couch, while the other hit Dexter square in the chest. Dexter fired too, a couple of shots in quick succession as he fell.

His ears still ringing from the shots, Wes jumped up and onto the couch next to Sam. He got ready to fire again. Myers was lying on his back, his gun in his right hand but pressed up against the couch, and all the fight was out of him. He tried to lift his arm but dropped the gun.

Wes glanced over at Dexter. He'd fallen against the reception desk and was dead. Mia was huddled against the wall at the side of the room, looking unhurt. It was only now that Wes looked down at Sam, whose head was slumped forward, a bullet hole in the side of his neck, blood pumping gently from the wound.

"I'm dying." It was Myers, and Wes saw that there was blood oozing out of his side just above the waist.

Wes jumped over the back of the couch, kicked the gun free, loosened Myers's shirt and pulled it up to look at the mess of a wound. The bullet had torn a shallow path through his oblique and exited again—despite all the blood, it didn't look like it had hit anything vital.

Wes glanced back at Dexter, still no signs of being anything but dead. Wes had never known him be much of a shot, but he'd fired off two rounds and still managed to hit his own boss in the neck.

"You're not dying. Come on, get to your feet."

Wes gave him a hand and helped him around and onto the other couch. He collapsed there, looking weakened by that brief exertion. Wes checked Sam for a pulse, then Dexter. And finally, he crouched down a few feet away from Mia.

"You okay?"

She stared back at him and nodded, apparently in shock. But then she glanced at Dexter's body and pointed.

"He was a *bad* man."

"Yeah, he was."

"I don't like to be touched."

"That's why I shot him."

She stared at him, laughed once, then again as she got the joke, or at least saw some humor in it.

"Can you get up?" She nodded and he said, "I just need to deal with something over here."

"Because you're a soldier."

"Kind of."

He moved back over to Brandon Myers.

Myers watched him approach, then closed his eyes.

"Just do it. I can't tell you anything, so just . . ." He choked on his words.

"What are you talking about? I have no argument with you." Myers opened his eyes, still with the look of someone who thought he was being tricked. "What have they told you about me?"

"They told me you don't take prisoners. Kyle told me . . ." He stopped, looked in the direction of Dexter's body, even though he wouldn't have been able to see it from there. "He told me that you're . . . well, just that you're a dangerous person to be around."

"Pretty rich coming from someone who just shot his own boss in the neck. And I'm flattered by the reputation-building, but I'm not the psycho they've painted me as. I'm just a regular guy who did a tough job in a complex theater." He pointed the gun at Myers. "Now, carefully, take out your phone and call Aaron Schalk."

Myers hesitated, then reached into his pocket for his phone and put the call through. Wes didn't know Schalk at all but he could tell from the brusque tone audible from the phone that he didn't go in for niceties.

As hurt as he was, Myers sounded nervous as he said to him, "Sir, I'm handing the phone over to James Wesley."

Wes took the phone and could hear Schalk talking, presumably thinking Myers was still on the line, though he'd fallen silent by the time Wes put the phone to his ear.

"Aaron Schalk?"

"Speaking. Care to explain, Mr. Wesley?"

"Short version is that Sam Garvey was a crook, working for an Iraqi warlord. He set me up, he killed my wife, and he did all of this to protect himself. Billy Tavares should be able to give you a fuller version." Wes noticed Myers react with shock—he'd obviously thought that Wes had killed Billy earlier in the day. "Garvey sent Zach Pine and two colleagues to kill me on my release from prison. I killed them. I killed Scottie Peters because he organized the suicide bombing that killed my wife—"

"*What?*"

"Really? If you didn't know about that, you might want to think about auditing all of your gray teams, because Madrid knew about it. So yeah, I killed him. I didn't kill Grace Burns or her friend. I didn't kill Billy Tavares. I didn't kill Brandon here, though he took a bullet in the side and you do need to get an ambulance out here pretty quick. I didn't kill Sam, though I did torture him a little and I would've killed him if Kyle Dexter hadn't beaten me to it with a spectacular piece of friendly fire. I killed Kyle. He deserved it. Oh, your team here also kidnapped and threatened to kill the daughter of the late General Nikola Pavić, and if that ever got out, the US would lose a *lot* of goodwill in this part of the world."

There was a pause after Wes finished, probably as Schalk tried to assimilate everything he'd just heard.

"What do you want?"

He sounded confused rather than hostile.

"I don't want anything. I want you to leave me alone. Like I said, Tavares and Myers will tell you what happened here, or most of it. I just spent three years in prison and I lost my ex-wife—I think I deserve a hell of a lot more, but all I'm asking of my country right now is that it leaves me alone."

There was another pause at the other end, stretching for a few seconds before the reply finally came.

"Okay."

"Good. If you're lying and you send anyone, you better send someone good, because if they try and fail I'll come after you and everyone else."

"I can't make open-ended promises, Wesley, but if your story stacks up, you won't have anything to fear from us."

"Okay, I'll take that."

"Wesley, before you go, I just want you to know, we had nothing to do with your son's disappearance, I'm certain of it. We've tried to trace him, but . . ."

"I guess Rachel didn't want us to find him. Maybe we should just respect that."

"Maybe you're right."

"I'll put you back on with Myers. He's lost a bit of blood."

He handed the phone back to a still shell-shocked Myers, then picked up his backpack and turned around to find Mia standing

234

waiting for him. He smiled, and they walked out of the office as Myers started to answer Schalk's questions.

Once they were on the street, Mia pointed and said, "It's this way." They started walking and then the sky above them danced with lightning. "There's going to be a thunderstorm! I loved them when I was little."

He wasn't sure why that didn't surprise him, but again, she'd moved on so quickly that he couldn't resist saying, "You sure you're okay?"

"Yes, I told you. That man was bad. He touched my face. But you killed him, so it's okay now."

"Yeah, I killed him."

"Like a soldier."

"Like a soldier."

She seemed remarkably untroubled by the experience, and as if to sum that up, she said, "Will you go to Milan now?" Her tone was as breezy and casual as if she'd asked him if he wanted to get some dinner.

He looked at her and smiled. "You know why I have to go there, right?"

"Because your son is there."

He nodded. His son was in Milan. A son he hadn't even known about until a few weeks ago, but still his. And once more he wished that he could speak to her, to tell her she didn't need to worry, that he got it now, that he finally understood.

# Forty

Wes took the elevator up the side of the Duomo, then joined the rest of the tourists as they filed along the open-air walkways and climbed the steps amid ornately carved pinnacles and flying buttresses. Finally he emerged onto the roof itself, the main spire clad in scaffolding at the far end, tourists walking about or sitting on the two sides sloping down gently from the apex.

He was there for a couple of minutes, looking out across the city and down at the square far below, before he realized Alina Manzoni was already there. She approached him and kissed him on both cheeks before standing back.

"Hello, Wes. I'm so sorry about everything that's happened."

"So am I."

She was ridiculously glamorous, ridiculously beautiful. She was dressed casually in jeans and sneakers and a striped T-shirt, her long hair catching in the slight breeze, and yet she still looked like a model in a photoshoot.

She looked around. "It's a beautiful place, isn't it?"

Wes nodded. It struck him as funny, that Mia had asked him a few times if he wanted to visit various churches and cathedrals with her, and here he was at last, albeit on his own.

"You know there's a rumor that this cathedral was dedicated to the devil?"

She smiled but didn't respond. She was Milanese, after all, so she probably knew more about it than Wes did.

"How did you know to look for me?"

"When you met with Rachel, wherever it was, you brought her a postcard of this place. It was among the belongings left in her hotel room safe in Granada. I wondered if she'd left it there as a message, but I doubt it somehow."

Alina nodded. "We met in Barcelona. She took the train with Ethan. I flew in, but took the train home. We had the paperwork ready—you know Roberto's a lawyer—so it was actually quite easy. And it was the way she wanted."

"She knew they were gonna kill her?"

"No, I don't think so. She feared that might be the case. She knew she was getting close to the truth about what happened to you. She had one person she needed to meet, the final piece of the puzzle. The idea was to leave Ethan with us for a few weeks, and seeing the way she was in Barcelona, I think she honestly believed she would come back for him."

He couldn't imagine the pain Rachel would have experienced if she hadn't believed that. How could she have handed over the son she'd so desperately wanted, believing she'd never see him again?

"But you said she completed the paperwork."

"A precaution, just in case, like writing a will. She knew we couldn't have children of our own, so it was easy for us—he's such a sweet boy."

"Well, I'm sure I wasn't a monster from the beginning either."

She laughed, but then saw he was being serious and said, "You're not a monster, Wes. It's true, there's something . . . detached in you. She often talked about it, but she also said it was just part of the work you did, the way you were trained."

Wes had thought that himself in the past, but he knew now that it wasn't true—the things he'd heard in the last few days had been enough to remove the scales from his eyes. Maybe Patrice had been made into the man he'd become, but Wes had been born with it already inside of him.

He shook his head. "She was being diplomatic, or she was lying. And I'm mad that she put herself in danger like that. I wasn't worth it."

"She thought so."

"Not enough to entrust our son to me. He *is* my son?"

"Of course." She smiled, full of love for the child. "He looks so much like you. It worried her at times, but he's really so sweet-natured, so loving . . ." She stopped, perhaps seeing the implications of what she was saying. "It wasn't that she didn't trust you to . . . You know, she thought you would be in prison for another two years, and even then, she couldn't be sure."

It hadn't been that, and Wes knew it. Rachel had loved him—it was the only explanation for why she'd tried so hard to clear his name. He'd loved her too once, as much as he knew how to love anyone, and it still troubled him that he'd so easily learned not to love her during his time in prison.

She had loved him, but she'd loved her son more, as was only natural, and in the event of her own death, she'd wanted to protect that sweetness of character she saw in Ethan. Ironically, Rachel, too, had been possessed of some of the same cold detachment as Wes, just enough to analyze her options with a cool gaze. She'd known exactly what she was doing.

"How safe are you at the moment, Wes?" He looked at her questioningly. For the first time, he noticed that Alina was nervous. Not scared like the people he'd encountered these last weeks, but fearful in a different way. "I mean, I know legally your sentence was cut, but you think they killed Rachel, so, I just wonder—"

"Alina, I'm not gonna take him from you. I don't know how safe I am, but that has nothing to do with it. I want him to be

Rachel's son, not mine—I'm not . . . Well, she knew what she was doing, that's all there is to it. She knew."

It was only now that he could see how much this meant to her. She started to cry and he held her for a minute while she sobbed and thanked him again and again. Even after these few weeks, she'd been so afraid of losing Ethan, and it was amazing for him to experience her relief. He'd thought of Mia as being alien, and yet he felt that way himself now, like someone who didn't fully understand normal human emotions, a sensation that only reinforced that he'd made the right decision.

And, unexpectedly, he thought again of sitting many years ago on that hillside in rural Georgia, the pale and stony landscape stretching out before him, the car lying on its roof and the little girl screaming and screaming. He didn't feel like he was that person anymore, but in truth, he couldn't be sure. Maybe that person would always be within him.

Alina broke away but held onto his hands.

"But we can keep in touch, yes?"

"Of course. And if you ever decide you can't . . ."

He stopped, because looking at her face, so suffused with love, he knew she'd never change her mind about this arrangement, about the gift her best and oldest friend had bestowed upon her. She turned now, looking across the rooftop, and waved at someone she saw there.

Wes looked too, and saw a young woman at the far end of the cathedral roof, up on the sloped surface with a very small boy. He didn't know why it had never occurred to him, that she might bring Ethan along.

"Is that him?"

He looked at the little figure, pointing something out to the woman, presumably a nanny. And Wes couldn't see him clearly from that distance but he was instantly overcome, emotion swelling up inside him, full of curiosity and nerves and longing—

"You want to meet him?"

She was about to raise her hand again, but Wes was quick to say, "No! No." He smiled at her. "I guess I'm a little human after all. I'll be able to walk away from here, Alina, because I know it's what Rachel wanted me to do, but I'm not sure I'll be able to do that if I know what I'm walking away from. Not yet. It's better this way."

"I understand."

She hugged him again, pulling tight, but then he broke away and stepped back, once, then again, and avoided looking toward the other end of the roof.

"Thanks, Alina."

She looked quizzically. "You're thanking me?"

"Yeah. I'm thanking you, for being there for her, for being a friend." He took another step away. "Take care."

"You too. Bye, Wes."

He turned and walked away, and when he found a line of people waiting for the elevator, he descended by the steps instead, wanting to remove himself as quickly as possible from the temptation of ruining other people's lives.

And he didn't look back at the cathedral as he walked away from it, even as he wondered if they were still up there on the roof, if Alina might be holding Ethan close and pointing to the square far below and the tiny people coming and going.

He was struggling even now against an urge to turn back. He thought he'd done the best thing for his son's future, but he couldn't be sure. Would Ethan grow up bitter and resentful knowing that Wes had left him? Maybe, but what chance would he ever have with Wes? Rachel had answered that question—it was why she'd made the decision for him, and why he had to stick with it and keep walking.

He walked all the way back to the hotel and into the ornate lobby lounge, where tea was being served. It was full of highly maintained Italians and Russians, stylishly dressed, many of them surrounded by shopping bags from the expensive stores nearby.

Then he saw Mia and he instantly felt more at peace with himself. A tiered afternoon tea was sitting on the table in front of her, untouched. She smiled when she saw him, and as he sat down she picked up the teapot.

"Shall I pour?"

"Sure."

The idea of pouring tea seemed to entertain her somehow, and she was smiling to herself as she said, "Did you see your ex-wife's friend and your son?"

"Yes, I did. He'll be staying with them."

"Sugar?"

"No, thanks."

She placed his teacup in front of him. "Where shall we go now?"

He idly took one of the dainty sandwiches and placed it on a plate. He didn't feel much like eating but he didn't want Mia to have an excuse to abstain. And it pleased him when she, too, took a sandwich.

"I have to go to Switzerland, just to visit the bank. It's actually not far from here. But after that, I'm not sure."

"I liked the black people."

He couldn't help but laugh a little.

"You mean Patrice's friends, in Lisbon?"

"Yes."

"Okay. So maybe after Switzerland we can go back to Lisbon."

"Really?"

"Why not. We have to be somewhere."

She smiled broadly. For a moment he thought she was going to hug him, but of course, she didn't. Instead, she took a bite from her sandwich, still smiling, and then she reached out with her other hand and pushed the bible along the banquette toward him.

He pulled the bookmark, opening the bible there on the seat rather than picking it up. He read the words that had been underlined and nodded to himself.

*Be not forgetful to entertain strangers: for thereby some have entertained angels unawares.*

Yes, maybe there was some truth in that—life was full of unexpected turns. He had no idea what the future held, just as he had no way of predicting whether he'd made the right decision for Ethan, so maybe it was pointless even to think about it.

A month or so back, a random assortment of people had stopped by a quiet café on a peaceful sunny morning. A mother and her child, a college couple, a young man with dreams of becoming a spy, a woman writing postcards to herself. They had all stopped there and they had died as a result. There was no planning for that.

He guessed all anyone could ever do was make the right choice in the moment. And in this moment, Wes believed he'd made the right choice. So they would finish their tea, and tomorrow they would make for Switzerland and then Lisbon, and they would keep going like that, for as long as the road opened up before them.

# Acknowledgments

Thanks, as ever, to my agent, Deborah Schneider, and everyone at Gelfman Schneider/ICM Partners. Thanks also to Laura Deacon and the superb team at Thomas & Mercer. And thanks, finally, to my readers, old and new, who make all of this possible—I dedicate this book to you.

# About the Author

Kevin Wignall is a British writer, born in Brussels in 1967. He spent many years as an army child in different parts of Europe and went on to study politics and international relations at Lancaster University. He became a full-time writer after the publication of his first book, *People Die* (2001). His other novels are *Among the Dead* (2002); *Who is Conrad Hirst?* (2007), shortlisted for the Edgar Award and the Barry Award; *Dark Flag* (2010); *The Hunter's Prayer* (2015, originally titled *For the Dogs* in the USA), which was made into a film directed by Jonathan Mostow and starring Sam Worthington and Odeya Rush; *A Death in Sweden* (2016); *The Traitor's Story* (2016); *A Fragile Thing* (2017); and *To Die in Vienna* (2018).